"Do you really ———— *——— ort of person who would plunk down a small fortune and move in next door to you a week before your wedding just to drive you nuts?"*

Maddy stood up slowly, looked Joe full in the face. Pronounced every word carefully. "I loved you, Joe," she said quietly. "But you didn't trust me. Not enough to tell me the truth."

Now Joe felt his temper rising, the temper he had thought had cooled long ago, to be replaced by the damning knowledge that, if he were to become rich beyond his dreams—and he had—he would never be happy, complete, without Maddy by his side. He had to love her. If he didn't, he was just plain nuts to be putting himself back into a position where she could cut his knees, and heart, right out from underneath him.

And still, he couldn't help himself....

THE
CHANDLERS
Request...

Marrying Maddy (SR#1469)
Jessie's Expecting (SR#1475)
Raffling Ryan (SR#1481)

Dear Reader,

Silhouette's 20th anniversary celebration continues this month in Romance, with more not-to-be-missed novels that take you on the romantic journey from courtship to commitment.

First we revisit STORKVILLE, USA, where a jaded Native American rancher seems interested in *His Expectant Neighbor*. Don't miss this second book in the series by Susan Meier! Next, *New York Times* bestselling author Kasey Michaels returns to the lineup, launching her new miniseries, THE CHANDLERS REQUEST.... One bride, *two* grooms—who will end up *Marrying Maddy*? In *Daddy in Dress Blues* by Cathie Linz, a Marine embarks on his most terrifying mission—fatherhood!—with the help of a pretty preschool teacher.

Then Valerie Parv whisks us to a faraway kingdom as THE CARRAMER CROWN continues. *The Princess's Proposal* puts the lovely Adrienne and her American nemesis on a collision course with...love. The ever-delightful Terry Essig tells the tale of a bachelor, his orphaned brood and the woman who sparks *A Gleam in His Eye*. Shhh.... We can't give anything away, but you *must* learn *The Librarian's Secret Wish*. Carol Grace knows...and she's anxious to tell you!

Next month, look for another installment of STORKVILLE, USA, and THE CHANDLERS REQUEST...from *New York Times* bestselling author Kasey Michaels. Plus, Donna Clayton launches her newest miniseries, SINGLE DOCTOR DADS!

Happy Reading!

Mary-Theresa Hussey

Mary-Theresa Hussey
Senior Editor

Please address questions and book requests to:
Silhouette Reader Service
U.S.: 3010 Walden Ave., P.O. Box 1325, Buffalo, NY 14269
Canadian: P.O. Box 609, Fort Erie, Ont. L2A 5X3

Marrying Maddy

KASEY MICHAELS

Silhouette
ROMANCE™
Published by Silhouette Books
America's Publisher of Contemporary Romance

For Maryanne Colas,
for being there

SILHOUETTE BOOKS

ISBN 0-373-19469-2

MARRYING MADDY

Copyright © 2000 by Kasey Michaels

This edition published by arrangement with Harlequin Books S.A.

® and TM are trademarks of Harlequin Books S.A., used under license.
Trademarks indicated with ® are registered in the United States Patent
and Trademark Office, the Canadian Trade Marks Office and in other
countries.

Visit Silhouette at www.eHarlequin.com

Printed in U.S.A.

Books by Kasey Michaels

KASEY MICHAELS,

a *New York Times* bestselling author of more than two dozen books, divides her creative time between writing contemporary romance and Regency novels. Married and the mother of four, Kasey's writing has garnered the Romance Writers of America's Golden Medallion Award and the *Romantic Times Magazine*'s the Best Regency Trophy.

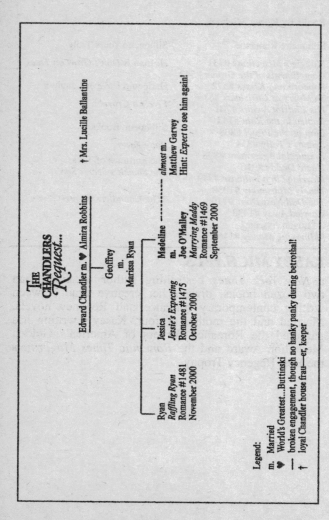

The
CHANDLERS
Request...

Edward Chandler m. ♥ Almira Robbins   † Mrs. Lucille Ballantine

Geoffrey
m.
Marissa Ryan

Madeline - - - - - - - - - - - *almost* m.
m.   Matthew Garvey
Joe O'Malley   Hint: *Expect to see him again!*
Marrying Maddy
Romance #1469
September 2000

Jessica
Jessie's Expecting
Romance #1475
October 2000

Ryan
Raffling Ryan
Romance #1481
November 2000

Legend:
m.   Married
♥   World's Greatest...Buttinski
- - -   broken engagement, though no hanky panky during betrothal!
†   loyal Chandler house frau——er, keeper

Chapter One

The midafternoon sun filtered through sheer white draperies that hung at a half-dozen nearly floor-to-ceiling windows in the corner bedroom on the third floor of the Chandler mansion.

The June heat barely registered in the electronically filtered, air-conditioned atmosphere that was busily sucking dust motes out of the air as quickly as the sun could highlight them.

Dark cherry furniture, all genuine antiques, was scattered around the room; a grouping of chairs and a small, overstuffed ivory couch placed in front of the marble fireplace. A high, four-poster bed was angled into one corner and backed by a living forest of potted plants, a tall, Oriental screen tucked into the greenery.

Three crystal chandeliers hung from the high, stuccoed ceiling. There was a vanity table that definitely lived up to its name, displaying enough mirrors and pretty cut-glass bottles with expensive labels to keep Snow White's stepmama too busy to look for poison apples.

There were original oil paintings on the walls of the bedroom, even on the walls of the huge bathroom that held a marble tub that had been brought over from France forty years earlier, so enormous it probably could have been floated across the Atlantic with a three-man crew aboard.

There was a separate dressing room, a separate showering room, both a built-in sauna and a mini beauty salon. The four-in-one walk-in closet—one large section for each season—was larger than most living rooms.

The remainder of the apartment, for this was only a small part of it, took up half of the third floor: a living room, formal dining room, full kitchen, a large guest bedroom and maid's quarters.

It comprised only one half of one floor of a three-million-dollar mansion. But, hey, be it ever so humble, it was home.

Back to the bedroom...dragging the eye from the huge poster bed, the fireplace mantel that had once resided in the Earl of Coventry's summer house on the isle of Jersey, the massive chandeliers...and to the trio of women gathered near the tall, three-sided mirror Madame Pompadour herself had once preened in front of before the ball.

One woman was seated on a straight-back Chippendale chair that had been moved across the carpet solely for the purpose of holding her body as she held sway over the situation. In other words, it would take no more than two seconds to play and win the game of "who's the boss?" if anyone were to ask.

The woman was a deceptive seventy; the sort that looks fifty, laughs like forty and can't believe she isn't still thirty. A tiny woman, no more than three inches over five feet, she probably didn't outweigh the chair she sat on as if it were a throne. Her perfectly coiffed light brown hair was piled high on her head above a long neck and a chin that was only slightly soft—three face-lifts, one eye job and a forehead lift just last year.

The manicured fingers of her right hand clasped a crystal sherry glass, half full. Her day dress was a soft blue silk paisley and she wore her skirt to the knee, because her legs were still slim, without a single telltale vein showing beneath her nude panty hose.

This woman, the clear matriarch of the Chandler family, spent a half hour each day with her legs inelegantly raised above her head in a yoga position in order to "reverse the damages of blood flow and gravity." That, however, was a family secret revealed only to her two granddaughters, who had caught her in this ignoble position and threatened to tell their grandfather on her.

But enough of Almira Chandler, and on to the other two women.

The second, Mrs. Ballantine—and *always* Mrs. Ballantine, even after twelve years as the Chandler housekeeper—stood to one side of the trio, a part of the scene, but really not a part of the small group.

Nearly six feet tall, all of it straight as a poker, and with an air of command about her that would have made her the terror of the second grade if she hadn't decided the classroom wasn't for her, Mrs. Ballantine wore bright red lipstick, and was secretly proud of her coal-black hair. She had the pale complexion of a person who hadn't been out in the sun since the Eisenhower administration.

At the moment, the formidable Mrs. Ballantine had a mouthful of straight pins.

And now to the last occupant of the room. This could only be Ms. Madeline Chandler, whose rooms these were, and who stood uncomfortably in front of the mirror, inspecting her reflection as the other two women watched.

The wedding gown she wore was nothing short of spectacular. It had rich, luxurious peau de soie. It had costly Alencon lace. It had cleverly positioned ribbons and silk flowers worked into the full, dropped-waist skirt, tucked into small "pockets" of material in the huge, off-the-shoulder "poof" sleeves. It had a long, flowing train both the flower girl and ring bearer could picnic on as the bride walked down the aisle.

Right now, the gown also had her, and Madeline Chandler was feeling rather trapped and smothered inside all of this beauty, inside all that it meant.

She thought about this for a moment, thought that her feelings were somehow wrong, and then worried that, for as trapped and smothered as she felt, she couldn't seem to do anything about it. Couldn't really even *care* all that much about it.

And she should. Shouldn't she?

"You look like a fairy princess. Except for the frown. Surely you aren't practicing to be the Wicked Witch of the West. I mean, remember, Maddy, dear, she wore black. Not white. More like Mrs. Ballantine." Almira Chandler, known as Allie to her grandchildren, looked to the housekeeper, shivered.

"Yes, much more like our own dear Mrs. Ballantine, who is looking remarkably like a porcupine at the moment."

"It's not white, Allie. It's ivory. With a hint of blush. Very 'in' this year, and all of that," Maddy explained. She looked into the full-length mirror again, drawing in her breath on a deep sigh that lifted her shoulders, then let both her mouth and her shoulders sag on the exhale. "I don't know, Allie," she said, shaking her head. "What do you think? Is this really *me*?"

"Is it you standing there, or is the gown really you? Clarify, Maddy darling. Always clarify. Mrs. Ballantine? More sherry, if you please? Being an observer seems to be thirsty work."

As Mrs. Ballantine plucked the glass from Almira's hand and walked toward a table bearing several crystal decanters, Maddy plucked at the skirt of the gown that had cost as much as her grandmother's first house, forty-five years earlier.

"The gown, I suppose," Maddy corrected. "I mean, I *like* it. Really. But do I really need three petticoats? I look like a mushroom. I wish I was taller, like Jessie. And less round. Maybe once the alterations are complete..."

"And you have the headpiece on, and your makeup, and your hair out of that rather inappropriate ponytail, and Matthew is on your arm..."

Maddy inspected her reflection—the heavy, blue-black hair pulled back from her full, yet slightly sharp-chinned face, the huge green eyes that looked so shadowed, so sad—not bridelike at all.

She bit her lips between her teeth, trying to bring some color into them, tipped her head to one side as she gripped both sides of her rather surprising twenty-three-inch waist. The gown really was beautiful. She wasn't so bad herself, except for that frown line between her eyes. She smiled, knowing it looked more like a grimace.

"Yes," she said at last, turning in a half circle, to look at the back of the gown as it was reflected in the mirror. "That's probably it. I'm missing the accessories."

"How wonderful. I'll be sure to tell Matthew," Almira said, winking at the unsmiling Mrs. Ballantine. "I'm sure he'll be delighted to have been reduced to a bridal accessory. Not that he isn't, of course. Other than to answer the minister at the correct times, he's nothing more than a convenient prop to hang the bride on the whole day. Poor boy."

Mrs. Ballantine stepped forward, and motioned for Maddy to step up onto the stool she had earlier placed on the carpet. *"Hemmm, hemm,"* she mumbled, still making small shooing motions to Maddy.

Almira chuckled. "What was that, Mrs. Ballantine? Him? Them? Oh, oh. *Hem.* You want to pin the hem? Goodness, woman, why didn't you just say so? You could have hurt yourself, you know."

The pins were removed from the wide red mouth. "Ha," Mrs. Ballantine barked out, showing her lack of amusement. Then she knelt on the carpet, put the pins back between her lips once more and got to work.

"I think Mrs. Ballantine is just so sweet, insisting on doing the alterations herself, not trusting the bridal salon to do them properly. Don't you, dear?"

Maddy turned to answer her grandmother, which earned her a sharp tug on the skirt of her gown, which nearly toppled her off the stool. "Sorry, Mrs. Ballantine. I shouldn't move, should I? And I am very grateful for all your help. We all are."

The pins transferred from mouth to hem, Mrs. Ballantine crowed, "Fall apart without me, the whole bunch of you," even as Almira now exchanged winks with Maddy's reflection in the mirror. "Told the old man I'd watch over you, and watch over you I will, even if it kills me outright." She glared at Almira for a moment, then added, "And it just might," then stuck more pins between her lips.

"You know, Mrs. Ballantine," Almira said, pausing to take another sip of sherry, "with all the long, fairly involved conversations my late husband and I had during his last illness five years ago, I truthfully cannot remember him mentioning your name a single time. How odd that he didn't bother to tell me that he'd appointed you guardian of us all, helpless creatures that we are. Even odder, don't you think, was that he made sure to include a *thank you and have a happy retirement* gift of money for you in his will."

Mrs. Ballantine pulled the pins from her mouth. "Wedding's in a week. Are we going to talk, or are we going to pin up this hem?" she asked, her tone clearly indicating that she didn't have time for idle chitchat.

"Oh, we'll pin the hem, Mrs. Ballantine. Definitely. Maddy? Stand still, darling. After all, the woman's armed."

Maddy bit her lips again, this time to keep from giggling. The running feud between her grandmother and Mrs. Ballantine was probably what kept the old lady so young, so spry. Between the two women, they had loved Edward Chandler with all their hearts, in different ways, for different reasons.

That Edward Chandler had believed Mrs. Ballantine the reincarnation of his old, hated Army sergeant was a secret he'd shared only with his family. Through guilt at the woman's obvious grief at Edward's death, or because they were all afraid of her, the family had gone along with Mrs. Ballantine's declaration that she had promised her late employer she would never leave, never desert the Chandler family.

After all, as Almira always said, who else would have the woman anyway? Mrs. Ballantine was about as appealing as prune whip on a stick.

"Mrs. Chandler? Please excuse the intrusion. The florist is on the telephone in my office. Something about trying to explain to you, one more time, why he can't dye six dozen pots of mums blue."

"How ridiculous. They can put a man on the moon, can't they? So why can't they do a simple little thing like—oh, never mind." Almira sighed, slapped at her knees and rose to her feet. "Thank you, Sarah," she said to her social secretary. "I suppose I can now safely leave you two to your own devices?" she asked Maddy and Mrs. Ballantine. Then, before either could answer, she swept out of the room, her stride smooth and graceful, even in three-inch heels.

"Fhought she'd neber lede."

"Pardon me, Mrs. Ballantine?" Maddy asked, turning to look down at the housekeeper, earning herself another sharp tug on her skirts for the effort.

Mrs. Ballantine pulled the pins from her mouth.

"I *said*, I thought she'd never leave. Now, what's the matter, Miss Maddy? And don't go telling me everything's fine, because it isn't. Never saw such an unhappy bride, or a grandmother so blind to what's smack in front of her face. Dratted woman. Probably had her head pulled too tight last year, and her brains have all shrunk."

"Mrs. Ballantine!" Maddy scolded, then laughed with real enjoyment—right up until she realized it was the first time she'd laughed in *real enjoyment* in quite a while. No, she wasn't being very bridelike, was she?

"I'm fine, Mrs. Ballantine. Honestly. Just some prewedding nerves. I imagine all brides get them. Now, I promise to stand very still while you finish pinning this huge hem."

"Going to take some time, you know."

"Yes, I know. I should have gone with the sheath, I suppose, but Allie did like this one so much."

"And you listened to her? Woman's an idiot."

"Yes, Mrs. Ballantine, I know," Maddy replied calmly, as the running feud between housekeeper and matriarch was as superficial as the women's regard for each other was deep. "She likes you, too."

Mrs. Ballantine lifted another half-dozen pins to her mouth, pausing only to say, "Now, think happy thoughts, Miss Maddy, as a bride should, and we'll be done here in about ten minutes. Then you can do something with that hair. At least the old lady was right about that. Ponytails are for children. Why, I remember..."

Maddy stared at her reflection as she allowed Mrs. Ballantine's words to glide over her head. And she remembered the last time she'd worn her hair in a ponytail. Where she had been, who had been there with her...

"You look gorgeous, Maddy. I think every bride should wear shorts, her hair pulled up like that. I mean, that veil and gown thing is definitely overdone. Now, what do you think of my groom gear?"

Maddy could see Joe O'Malley standing in front of her, just as he had stood in front of her eighteen months earlier. His smile was wide in his tanned, handsome face. His arms were out at his sides as he playfully turned himself in a half circle, inviting her to admire his cutoffs and bright red Phillies jersey, the number 32 stamped on the back in huge white characters.

He stopped moving, with his back to her, and smiled at her over his shoulder. Sandy hair much too long, but just right for him, slid down onto his forehead. His blue eyes sparkled with mischief. Physically the man was a near god, even in cutoffs. Maybe especially in cutoffs. He had great legs for a man. "Well, come on, Mad. Don't leave me hanging here. Am I a groom's groom, or what?"

"You're a nut," Maddy said, and he completed his fashionable "turn" before grabbing her close, kissing her senseless.

Joe O'Malley was very good at kissing Madeline Chandler senseless. Very good. It was one of his most adorable attributes.

It was also, most probably, what had led to the two of them standing outside the small white chapel on the Strip in Las Vegas, ready to recite their vows to each other in front of God and an Elvis impersonator.

Possibly not the best reason to marry someone,

but not that bad a reason, not when you got right down to it. At least that was what Maddy had convinced herself. Was still trying to convince herself, even as the sane, rational part of her—admittedly having been considerably downsized since meeting Joe—fought to maintain some sort of control.

Because, although a smiling Joe, a joking Joe, and a loving Joe were all wonderful, they'd had their share of disagreements. Even arguments. And those arguments most often concerned not the present, but the future. Her place in that future, his function in that future.

Even in the heat of Las Vegas, the heady excitement of an impromptu elopement, Maddy still had that small nagging *sane* part of her trying to throw a last-minute monkey wrench into her happiness.

Which probably meant something. Something like, hey, maybe postponing this wedding until they'd worked out a few things. Like, where they would live. How they would live. Small stuff like that...

She put her hands on Joe's forearms, pushed him slightly away from her. And asked a question she didn't want to ask. "I heard the phone ring early this morning, while I was in the shower. Was it Larry?"

Joe nibbled at her left ear. "Um-hmm."

Maddy's knees were crumbling, but she wouldn't let them. She might be the youngest Chandler. She might have been hiding behind the door when the Chandler common sense had been handed out. But she did know when it became time to trust her instincts. And her instincts were telling her that Larry Barry and his lamebrained ideas showed all the signs of becoming the "other woman" in her marriage. "And Larry wanted what?"

Joe backed off a little, kissed the tip of her nose. But did not look into her eyes. "You know. Typical Larry stuff. We're brilliant, megatalented, and we're soon going to be rich, rich, rich. Right after we're done being poor, poor, poor, not that we talk about that part much." He took Maddy's hand, gave it a tug. "Come on, sweetheart, let's get married."

Maddy's feet stayed firmly planted on the sidewalk. "How poor, poor, poor? You did something, didn't you, Joe? I can tell, because you're not looking at me. It's our wedding day, and you've barely looked at me, talked to me. What did you and Larry do?"

Joe sighed, stabbed his long, straight fingers through his hair. "Never could fool you, could I? Sometimes it's hard to believe we've only known each other for three months. Okay, Maddy. Larry and I both quit our jobs last week—"

"You did *what? Last week!*"

"Yeah, last week. That's why I could fly here to Vegas. We quit our jobs, cashed in our IRAs and any stocks and CDs we had, and we're going to risk it all on this one roll. You're now looking at one half of Barry and O'Malley Software. Incorporated, no less. It was going to be a surprise, a wedding present. Now, aren't you sorry you made me give away the surprise?"

"Oh God." Maddy walked away from him, turned in a full circle, glared at him, then walked back, not sure if she should give in to impulse and hit him, or just brush past him, keep on going. How could he do this to her? And today of all days!

Joe put his hands on her shoulders, gave her a small, encouraging shake. "Come on, Mad, don't look like the world is coming to an end. You know this new idea of mine is going to fly. Bill Gates isn't the only guy who can get an idea, you know. And Steve Jobs. Those guys started out working out of their own garages, and now look at them."

Maddy ignored the sales pitch, as she'd heard it all before. They'd argued about all of it before, again and again. Joe was the computer genius, Larry the businessman. Together, they were going to conquer the world.

"Let me get this straight, Joe. You quit your job, liquidated all your holdings and went into business with Larry Barry the Loser? A week before you knew we were going to come here and maybe be married? When were you going to tell me all of this? Oh, yes, it was to be a surprise. You were going to tell me while we were on our honeymoon. Which will be in a cardboard box under a bridge, by the sound of it."

Joe's full, sensuous mouth flattened into a thin, white line. "If this is another way of saying, yet again, that we could live very comfortably on your trust fund, Mad, I'm not buying it, okay?"

"*Okay,* and I'm not *Mad.* Makes me sound like a wild animal that should be put down." She broke free of him, turned her back on him once more. "I must be out of my tiny little mind. Allie said so, said I should bring you home, let her meet you before I did anything impetuous. Said I should take my time, not rush into anything. Why do I never listen to her?"

She felt Joe's hand on her shoulder. "Do you

want to listen to her, Maddy? Or is it just that you don't believe in me? I love you, Maddy. I've loved you since the moment I first saw you. You know that, and you love me, too. I'd never do anything to hurt you.''

Maddy wanted to raise her own hand, place it on top of his. She wanted to lean back, lean against his hard strength. Fall back into the fantasy.

But she didn't. She stepped out from under his hand, turned to face him, tears stinging her eyes.

''No, Joe. You'd never do anything to hurt me. Not on purpose. You'd only make plans for both our lives, without telling me. This isn't going to work, Joe. I'm not a gambler, not in Las Vegas, certainly not with my life. And I'm not used to poverty. I don't even know how to boil water, let alone how to keep a house. Or a cardboard box. We'd hate each other within a month.''

She watched through tears as Joe's eyelids lowered, as the glitter of—could it be tears?—entered his own eyes. ''So that's it? One small stumbling block and it's so long, Joe, been nice to know you? Five minutes away from getting married, and you're going to run away, run back to your cushy life and all that old-money security? Is that love, Maddy? Is that trust?''

The tears spilled down Maddy's cheeks now as she stood in front of the mirror, watching them drip off her chin, fall onto her wedding gown. All as she stood smack in the middle of the life she had always known, the one Joe had asked her to give up in order to figuratively jump off a bridge with him, into Lord only knew what sort of future.

She wasn't a snob, damn it all! She wasn't a rich

brat, spoiled and selfish. At least that was what she'd been telling herself for the past eighteen months, ever since leaving Joe standing outside the wedding chapel and flying home to Pennsylvania.

She was a sane, semi-levelheaded human being, one who knew that only disaster awaited a marriage entered so hastily, with a man who acted without consulting her, a man who would "risk it all on this one roll."

Was what she had felt for Joe love? Did that love have anything to do with trust? "No, Joe," she whispered, "it wasn't either of those things. It couldn't have been. What we had was a dream, only a dream. A dream and a passion for each other that we mistook for love. It's too late for us now, for so many, many reasons. But this time—this time, Joe— I'm going to get it right."

"Did you say something, Miss Maddy?" Mrs. Ballantine asked as she stood behind her, fluffing out the long train.

"Yes. I was talking to myself, Mrs. Ballantine," Maddy said, trying to smile. "Must be another part of prewedding jitters."

"I don't know. Living with your grandmother is enough to have anyone talking to herself," Mrs. Ballantine said. "Now, stand still while I figure out how to bustle this thing. We want everything just right, don't we?"

"Yes, Mrs. Ballantine," Maddy agreed, quickly wiping the tears from her face. "We certainly do want everything to be just right...."

Chapter Two

The fitting finely completed, Maddy gratefully allowed Mrs. Ballantine to help her out of the heavy gown and then went wandering off to take her second shower of the day. The underslips itched, and she'd actually broken out in a few hives along her waistline.

Mrs. Ballantine promised to cover the waistbands with some soft cotton, but Maddy still itched, so a cool shower sounded pretty good to her.

Hives. She never broke out in hives. It was pretty pitiful, being allergic to your own wedding gown. Not prophetic, she was sure. Just pitiful.

Her hair still in the ponytail, and only slightly damp around the edges from the shower, Maddy dressed in a short denim skirt and a pink-and-red flowered denim vest with metal snap closings she'd picked up on sale the previous week.

She loved sales, couldn't get enough of them, especially considering that she hadn't looked at a price tag until eighteen months ago. Now paying retail was an anathema to her, buying on credit felt like something akin to mortal sin and, as she'd discovered the delights of the local malls, she'd also developed a healthy appetite for fast food and huge pretzels slathered with mustard.

She knew her family thought she had probably gone a little overboard in her zealousness for economy, her pursuit of cooking and other household skills, even her recently discovered passion for gardening.

Matt was going to get himself one very accomplished wife, the lucky dog. Not that millionaires probably cared all that much about cents-off coupons and buying in bulk.

But, small as her accomplishments must look when compared to those of her older, quite successful siblings, Maddy was happy with her life.

Well, with most of her life.

She sure wished she didn't have hives. They weren't a good sign, definitely. The first and last time she'd had hives was on the airplane, flying home from Nevada. They'd started on her face, and hadn't quit until she was all but covered in the itchy things.

Nerves, the Chandler family doctor had declared when he'd met her in the local emergency room an hour after her flight touched down. He then treated her with antihistamines and the recommendation that she look inside herself and discover what could be troubling her, as her body was merely reacting to her stress in its own particular way. That was Dr. Neally, full of holistic ideas and the patient having the power to cure herself. The man even had a lava lamp in his waiting room.

Maddy had taken the antihistamines, and switched doctors. Her new physician, Dr. Linda Garvey, Matt's sister, told her pretty much the same thing, but then said she should sit down, examine her life and decide what she wanted from it. For some reason, what Maddy decided she wanted was to learn how to cook. And she ran with it, straight to classes at the local community college.

She hadn't had a hive since, thanks to her soon-to-be sister-in-law.

Until today, damn it. And she'd rather stick one of Mrs. Ballantine's straight pins in her eye than call the way-too-insightful Linda for help. Not when she was supposed to be the happy bride, only a week shy of her wedding to her doctor's brother.

Maddy found some antihistamine capsules in her kitchen and downed two, even knowing that they'd make her sleepy in the middle of the day. She slipped her bare feet into a pair of cherry-red sneakers gotten for twenty percent off at JCPenney's, and headed down the front stairs to see what the rest of the family was doing.

Ten minutes later she was sitting on the carpet in the second drawing room, surrounded by boxes, ribbons and tissue paper, once more playing Happy Bride. And trying to ignore the itch that seemed to be crawling up her back.

Jessica Chandler, Maddy's older sister, sat cross-legged on the Oriental carpet with her, the two of them in the center of the room surrounded by white linen covered tables displaying many of the wedding gifts as they opened today's deliveries.

At least one of the gifts was always good for a laugh.

"Ah, just what you need most, Maddy," Jessica said, holding up the unwrapped gift. "Another silver tray. What does that make now—ten of them? You'd think *somebody* would have some imagination, wouldn't you?"

"Great-Aunt Harriet has some," Maddy replied, warily eyeing the object in her hands. "What *is* this?"

Jessie laughed out loud. "And we have today's winner. What is it, Maddy? I don't know, wait—it's Great-Uncle Albert!" she suggested, still giggling. "I wouldn't lift the lid if I were you. Especially if you feel a sneeze coming on."

"Funny, Jessie, very funny." Maddy looked at the vase, or ornamental urn, or whatever the devil she held in her hands, then carefully placed it on the carpet, still unable to believe what she was seeing. Her chin began to itch, but she ignored that, too.

The "Thing" Great-Aunt Harriet had sent by messenger—Maddy already had decided to think of it as the "Thing"—stood at least two feet high, and was fashioned out of some sort of porcelain. And it had to be old as dirt, something Great-Aunt Harriet had pulled from her collection and forwarded to her great-niece instead of just sending her another silver tray, like any normal person.

The Thing had a lid, and the lid had a handle—two close-to-naked cherubs cavorting. The Thing also had side handles, both of them similarly unclothed cherubs bent forward at the waist, and looking as if they were about to do swan dives onto the floor.

She and Joe would have laughed and laughed—
no! She would *not* think of Joe O'Malley again.

She scratched at an annoying itch behind her
knee, and went back to inspecting her latest gift.

The Thing was so ugly, so overdone with intricate
scrollwork and rosy-cheeked cherubs, and even bits
of faux greenery, that Maddy was sure it had to be
worth a small fortune. Ugly things almost always
were. Worst of all, it seemed familiar; like something she'd at least seen a variation of during her
college studies.

Carefully removing the dome lid and placing it
back in the box, Maddy lifted the remaining piece
and inspected the bottom of the base. "*Nove,* with
an asterisk under it. Good Lord, Jessie, it's a *Le
Nove*. I should have known. I remember one from
my classes—covered in shells and painted with
mythological figures. Look, there are shells on this
one, too, along the base. Well, at least now I know
what to say in my thank-you note to Great-Aunt
Harriet."

"You sure do, Maddy. 'Dear Aunt Harriet, thank
you so much for the exquisite *Nove*. It will look so
lovely in the basement storage area.'"

Maddy rolled her eyes, even as she scratched at
her chin. "Jessie, this is a *Nove*. Straight from the
late 1700s. A true, if revolting, work of art. I
wouldn't put it in the *basement*. Great-Aunt Harriet
meant well, and always does." She replaced the lid,
tucked the vase back into its box. Then she smiled
evilly. "I'll give it to Allie."

"Only if you want to be cut out of my will, young
lady," Almira Chandler said as she walked into the
room, looked down into the tissue-filled box. "Did

I hear someone say Great-Aunt Harriet? For our twenty-fifth wedding anniversary, she sent back the silver compote your grandfather and I had given her one Christmas. That's Harriet, the idiot. Some people give gifts that keep on giving, or whatever. Harriet just keeps recycling the same old stuff. I imagine it makes some sort of sense—to her.''

"But you love her, Allie," Maddy said. "You love her because she's three years younger than you and looks ten years older. Like you've said, you just can't turn your back on a woman who makes you look so good at family parties.''

"Twenty years older than me, Maddy, not ten." Almira laughed as she peered down into the box. "Now, what did the idiot send over now? The woman's been cleaning house and stuffing up all her relatives' houses for the last decade, saying she's going to die any day and wants her *treasures* in loving hands first. Which," she ended, straightening, "explains that hideous Chelsea tea caddy Mrs. Ballantine keeps insisting on putting on the breakfast table. Just what I want to wake up to, certainly. A grinning idiot figure of a man with a round, bare belly and a lotus leaf for a hat. He even has *teeth*, for crying out loud. And Harriet will linger on another twenty years, until she's buried us all under her junk.''

"Very valuable junk, Allie, according to Maddy, our very own Art History major, although we probably should remember she graduated with only a *C* average," Jessie interjected, opening yet another box, pulling out yet another silver tray. "My, Maddy, this *is* your lucky day, isn't it?''

Maddy looked at her sister, slimmer than her,

taller by four inches, older by three years. Jessie had dark honey-brown hair as opposed to Maddy's own deepest black, pale blue eyes to her vibrant green. She was a bright, talented, successful young woman with a lifelong air of dignity and composure about her that Maddy had always envied, even as she had tagged after her, worshiping her.

Jessica was so confident, so sure of herself, and always had been. So successful, working side by side with their brother, Ryan, in the family business.

Maddy wished she could be more like her sister, rather than being the "baby" of the family, the one without a job, without a career, without, it seemed, much ambition or direction at all. And not expected to have any of those attributes, either, come to think of it.

If they'd had a Chandler family pet, they'd expect it to learn more tricks than they had ever expected from Maddy. No one in the family had batted a single eye or made a single comment when she'd withdrawn from her graduate courses, come home and learned how to cook pot roast. She sometimes wondered if she'd accepted Matt's proposal because she loved him, or because he, at least, seemed to think she had *some* sort of potential.

Not that Joe O'Malley hadn't thought she'd had potential. As a lover, that is. The asking her to be his wife part had only been an afterthought, she was sure. Something he thought he should do. Especially when he was about to lower the boom of his grand get-rich scheme. Having her safely married to him before she found out probably had seemed like a good idea at the time. The rat.

And now the rat was rich. Filthy rich. He didn't

need a little wife cutting coupons and sewing on buttons. Not that she had taken those courses just to make herself better equipped to be Joe's wife, if the man were to come to his senses and figure out he simply could not live without her. Not at all.

Maddy stuck out her tongue, swiped it over her top lip, which had begun to tingle ominously.

And not that she needed grad school or cooking classes to strike out on her own. She could be on her own if she wanted to. Sure, she could. She could be working in some small museum, or in an art gallery somewhere. She could be independent. But, no. She had to leave the classroom, go running off to elope with a man whose kiss was enough to make her forget everything but the man, the kiss.

Which had gotten her—where? Almost to the altar, that's where. With another man.

Maddy shook her head, banishing these pointless thoughts, knowing she had to stop using Joe as an excuse for her own failings. She hadn't wanted a career, and she knew it now just as she had known it then. Only she hadn't known what she wanted back then, and as Chandlers all went to college, she had gone to college. And gotten straight *C*'s, as Jessie had just pointed out.

She'd gotten straight *A*'s in all her classes at the community college. She loved her classes. That had to mean something. Had to mean more than that she had started taking the classes because Joe might come back and need a wife who knew how to cook. She *enjoyed* being domestic. Why, she'd even begun taking parenting classes last semester. Wasn't that how she and Matt had gotten together? Because of their shared interest in having a family?

What Maddy wanted, had always wanted, she could now acknowledge, was a husband to love, a man who loved her above and beyond anything else in his world. And babies—lots of them. A home of her own. Let Jessie and Ryan run the business, heap more millions into her trust fund. She'd always be grateful to them for it. But she would be more than content to stay home and bake brownies, which she did now, from scratch, after taking a bakery class at the community college.

Cooking classes, classes on handling a family budget, gardening classes, even one on flower arranging—she'd taken them all, excelled at them all. Enjoyed them all.

Her degree in Art History meant less than nothing to her, but she truly treasured the First Place blue ribbon she had won last fall at the Great Allentown Fair for her chocolate cheesecake.

Eighteen months after admitting to Joe that she couldn't boil water, Maddy had transformed herself into an accomplished cook, an enthusiastic gardener and a woman who actually knew how to hang wallpaper.

All so she could marry Matthew Garvey and have a house nearly as huge as this one, a staff to handle any emergency and enough free time to take every class the community college offered.

If there was something wrong with this, and Maddy was sure there was, she refused to recognize that she now had what it took to be a stay-at-home wife to a struggling young businessman, but she no longer had that struggling young businessman.

She unconsciously began to scratch at a spot behind her left ear.

"Maddy? *Maddy.* Allie's talking to you," Jessie said, giving her sister a playful shove in the ribs.

Maddy looked up at her grandmother, blinked a few times to clear her head and said rather dreamily, "Hmm?"

"Articulate as ever, darling," Almira said, shaking her head. "I *said,* there's a moving van next door. Mrs. Ballantine was nice enough to find your grandfather's binoculars for me, and I wondered if you two wanted to go into the morning room, which has such lovely *spying* windows?"

Maddy shook her head. "Allie! Don't tell me you actually want to spy on the new neighbors, see their furniture, probably make insulting cracks about every second piece that comes out of the truck."

"And there's something wrong with this?" Allie's smile faded even as her green eyes twinkled. "Don't let this miracle of plastic surgery fool you. I'm old now, Maddy, and just have to get my kicks wherever I can find them. So humor me, okay?"

Jessie was already on her feet. "Come on, Maddy, it'll be fun."

"For you, maybe," Maddy said, also getting to her feet. "But Matt and I wanted to buy that house, remember? If I'm going to scope out the new neighbors, I'd much rather do it with Grandad's old hunting rifle. Buying the place right out from under us like that, topping our bid with a *one-time* offer the Realtor couldn't refuse."

"I'm going to make you an offer you can't refuse," Jessie said, her voice rather muffled, as if she were speaking with marshmallows in her cheeks. "So, are you saying we've got nefarious characters moving into the old Harris house?"

"No, Jessie. What I'm saying is that I have next to no interest in our new neighbors. You and Allie go spy on them if you want. I'll be out back, checking on my roses." And taking a peek in the first mirror she saw on her way out, because her upper lip suddenly felt rather *fat*.

"Speaking of roses, I heard that the new owner is going to cut down all of Miriam Harris's rose gardens and replace them with a second tennis court, or something like that," Allie said as she walked away.

"What! How—how could they *do* that? Miriam's roses have been there for fifty years, at least." Maddy followed after Almira, nearly jogging to keep up with her grandmother's brisk steps, all thoughts of mirrors and her possibly fat lip banished. "I mean, are these people absolute *idiots?* Who needs two tennis courts?"

Mrs. Ballantine stood at attention in the hallway, conveniently armed with a huge pair of vintage World War II field glasses, which she wordlessly passed to Almira before stepping back to let the three women pass. To an observant person, the two women performed like a well-trained tag-team wrestling duo. But Almira's grandchildren weren't being all that observant right now. At least one of them wasn't, anyway.

"Who needs two tennis courts? I don't know, dear, why don't you look and see?" Almira answered, already in the mostly glass-sided morning room, the door closed behind them. Besides being the best vantage point to the driveway next door, the large, wicker-filled atrium was a family favorite for resting, and curling up with a good book.

Almira's husband had added the room as an anniversary present years ago, and the only solid wall in the room was taken up with floor-to-ceiling bookcases stuffed three deep with romance novels. Sarah had them all cross-indexed and alphabetized, and a small card catalog stood in the far corner. Almira Chandler was very serious about her cherished books. Very serious.

Almira shoved the binoculars into Maddy's hands—it was either take the things or have them jammed into her gut. "Why don't you take a peek, and then maybe you can tell me what an idiot looks like. Or didn't I mention that the owner is already on the property, overseeing the unloading of what looks to be a small mountain of boxes?"

Jessie, who had been watching all of this with a rather confused smile on her face—as she knew their grandmother never did anything without a reason—helpfully drew back the sheer curtains to give her sister a better view.

Maddy lifted the binoculars to her eyes, knowing that somehow she had been roped into doing what her grandmother wanted, again. She blinked as she saw nothing but fuzzy greenery through the lenses, then adjusted both the knob on the binoculars and her direction, slowly moving her sight along the sweep of lawn, past the white-painted split-rail fence covered in trailing red roses that divided the two properties.

Now more grass, trees and the start of the sweep of brick driveway that made a huge semicircle in front of the Harris house. She'd planned to plant white petunias and blue alyssum along both sides of that long driveway, as a complement to the blue-gray stone and creamy white wood trim of the house. With a couple of red geraniums mixed in, to pick up the dull red in the bricked driveway.

So many plans. So many things she was going to do with that house. Holding on to the heavy binoculars with only one hand, she used the other to run her fingernails over the wedge of bared flesh above her vest.

Feet. She saw feet. Male feet. Bare feet, standing on the brick driveway. Giving the powerful binoculars another small adjustment, she moved them slightly upward. Past remarkably straight legs, to a pair of khaki cutoffs and a white shirt with some sort of logo on it.

Too tiny to make out, even with the field glasses.

Maddy took a breath, moved the binoculars another fraction. Forgot about the itch on her chin.

"Joe."

She said his name calmly, as if she had been expecting to see what she now saw. Why, she didn't know. It had to be something about the knees, or something like that. Joe had great knees, not knobby at all. Her mind must have recognized them even before she saw his face. And now that mind had gone on Stun.

She didn't itch anymore. She could safely say that. Because she was suddenly *numb,* all over.

"Who, Maddy?"

"I think that's *whom,* Jessie, dear," Almira said, moving closer to Maddy. "Did you say Joe? I thought you said Joe. But you couldn't have said Joe, could you? I mean, what would that mean?"

Maddy was still staring through the binoculars, watching as Joe moved, pointed to a stack of boxes, said something to one of the workers. Smiled. Showed that single dimple in his left cheek. Made her heart flip over, land again with a sickening *thud*.

"I'm going to kill him," she announced quietly, matter-of-factly.

By now, Jessie understood what was happening. Not all of it, of course. But enough to know that trouble was coming—with a capital *T*. She grabbed the binoculars from her sister. "Joe? Joe O'Malley? *Your* Joe O'Malley? Ohmigod, Maddy! *Where?* Which one?"

"It doesn't matter, Jessie. He'll be dead before you can meet him."

Jessie squinted as she ran the binoculars over the figure of Joe O'Malley, at last getting a glimpse of the guy who had broken her sister's heart. "Wow, cute. No wonder you—well, never mind." Sorry she'd said what she said, she quickly passed the binoculars to Allie as she took hold of her sister's arm. "Now, Maddy…"

"I'm having a nightmare, aren't I?" Maddy said, shaking off Jessie's hand. "First Great-Aunt Harriet, and now Joe O'Malley. It has to be a nightmare. But, if I shoot him, I'll wake up. Why, the bang alone would wake me, right? That should work."

Almira hadn't used the binoculars, just placed them on a small table and walked toward the closed door leading to the hallway. She stood there, silently, her expression blank, and laid a hand on the doorknob.

"This way, darling," she said, opening the door as Maddy stomped around the room in circles, her fists clenched, her mind going in sixteen directions at once. "May I suggest the front door? It's the fastest way."

"*Allie*, for God's sake, don't *help* her," Jessie said in mingled exasperation and...could it be relief? No, that couldn't be it. She felt sorry for her baby sister. Truly she did.

"Why not, Jessie?" Maddy said as, at last, everything fell into place. Every little bit of what was happening to her at this moment. "She brought *him* here, didn't she?"

Almira Chandler put one fluttering, newly manicured hand to her chest. "*I* brought him here? Why, Madeline Chandler, shame on you. What *are* you saying?"

Maddy growled low in her throat, like an animal about to pounce, then straightened her shoulders and headed past her grandmother. "No, I don't have time for this. You I can kill any time. Joe first!"

Mrs. Ballantine slipped into the room, her head turned to watch as Maddy stomped down the hallway on the way to the front door. She waited until she could hear the door slam, wincing only slightly as the chandelier in the foyer tinkled a bit in the passing breeze.

"Shame on you, Mrs. Chandler," she said, shaking her head. "Bringing an old heartache into Miss Maddy's life just a week before her wedding to that nice Mr. Garvey. How could you have done such a thing to that poor little girl?"

"I don't know, Mrs. Ballantine, I really don't," Almira replied, sighing. "It must be this old age of mine. I just seem to do the most outlandish things."

Jessie looked from one woman to the other. Neither smiled. Neither allowed a single emotion to show on her face.

"Why, you two *sneaks!* You've been planning this together, haven't you?"

"Darling," Almira said reasonably, "Mrs. Ballantine and I can't even plan menus together, not without nearly coming to blows."

Jessie thought about this for a moment, then pointed her finger at her grandmother, then at Mrs. Ballantine. She opened her mouth, wagged her finger a time or two as she searched her brain for something to say, anything to say. And then she let her arm drop to her side and said simply, "Thank you."

"Whatever for?" Mrs. Ballantine said, looking as innocent as a drill sergeant could, which wasn't very much.

Jessie rubbed at her forehead, trying to tell herself that nothing had changed, nothing *would* change. Then her blue eyes widened as another thought struck her. "Allie? Mrs. Ballantine? You aren't going to say anything to Matt, are you? I mean, Maddy needs your help. Lord knows she's been a mess, especially since Joe O'Malley's company went public and his picture was on the cover of *Newsweek*—but you *aren't* going to meddle in *my* life, right? Right?"

Almira put a hand on Jessie's arm. "I don't meddle, Jessica. I never meddle. Why, I'm as surprised as you are that Joseph O'Malley bought the Harris house."

"Yeah. Right. Sure." Jessie kissed her grandmother's cheek. "You just keep on believing that Maddy and I believe that. And then keep your meddling out of *my* life."

Chapter Three

Joe O'Malley heard the faint echo of a slamming door coming from the direction of the Chandler house. He stood stock-still, pretended for a moment he could feel the concussion of moving air and then began to count silently in his head. *Twenty, nineteen, eighteen...*

When he got to *twelve,* he turned to one of the workmen. "I'm expecting someone shortly, Chad. Please just say I'm inside, okay?"

Chad lifted his Phillies cap and scratched his head. "How will I know who your visitor is?"

Joe shrugged. "Oh, I don't know, Chad. Smoke coming from her ears. Fire sparks shooting from her eyes. You'll figure it out."

"Oh, a woman. Well, that explains it," Chad said as Joe leisurely jogged toward the open door to his new house, stepping inside just in time to hear a rather angry bellow that had his name in it somewhere, right before the words "you dirty, rotten, *miserable*..."

He smiled, and headed for the massive kitchen. Food to soothe the savage beast, that was what he needed. He hoped this particular savage beast still liked peanut butter and jelly sandwiches.

He was just searching through a pile of cardboard boxes for a loaf of bread when Maddy skidded to a halt inside the kitchen. *"You."*

As openings went, that "you" was fairly ominous, and he hoped all his sharp knives were still lost somewhere inside a packing crate. He turned, slowly, and looked Maddy up and down, careful not to reveal to her how much he wanted to grab her, kiss her and make mad passionate love to her as soon as Chad and his buddies brought in the mattress.

God, how he had missed her. How he had lain awake nights, missing her. Spent his days missing her. Missing her smile, her soft mouth, her sweetly rounded body.

When he wasn't madder than hell at her, that is.

"You rang?" he drawled now, holding up the peanut butter jar, which was a pretty sad defensive weapon. "I've always wanted to say that. Oh, and what happened to your lip? You look like you ran into something."

There wasn't any steam coming out of Maddy's ears. That had to be good, not that he'd really expected to see smoke.

But he did see green fire, not red, flashing in her eyes. Emerald-green sparks, the sort that warned that a Maddy tornado was about to strike. And then, as if something he'd said had just filtered through the thoughts of mayhem skipping around in her brain, she brought a hand to her mouth, winced.

"Damn it! Damn you, Joe O'Malley, look what you've done to my lip!"

He leaned one hip against the counter. "Honey, I haven't had time to do that to your lip. But if you want the bottom one to match it, I'd be happy to volunteer my services. A few kisses, a little nibbling…some gentle sucking…"

She dropped her arm to her side, clenching both hands into fists. "Joe the great lover. Spare me, O'Malley."

He shrugged, careful not to smile. Or wince. "Hey, I tried. Now, is there anything else I can do for you? I'm kind of busy, moving in and all. But, as I was just about to make myself a sandwich anyway, I suppose the least I could do is feed you. Oh, and do you know you've got great big hives all over your neck? You look kind of polka-dotted, and kinda cute. Still, you probably ought to take something."

Maddy couldn't think of anything more to say now that the first, blind explosion of anger was behind her. Besides, she was out of breath from running all the way, she was covered in hives—which couldn't possibly add anything to her consequence, no matter what Joe said—and it was pretty hard to be cuttingly sarcastic when you could barely breathe and the man you wanted drawn and quartered was all but *goggling* at your chest as it heaved up and down with each breath.

And she was pretty sure he wasn't inspecting her for more hives.

"You 'ought my house," she said at last, her

softly pointed but at the moment rather bumpy chin thrust in his direction. That was pretty lame, certainly didn't convey all the emotions churning inside her, and she was having trouble pressing her lips together to form the letter *B*, but it would do for a start. "O'Malley, you 'ought my damn house!"

"Is this where I plead innocence, or just when I ask you what in hell you're talking about? I *ought* this house from the Harrises. Nice people, by the way. I met them this morning during closing on the property. They're moving to Arizona, you know. Something about golfing all year round…gardening in every season. Something like that. Um, maybe you should sit down, Maddy. You're not looking too good."

You are, she thought to herself, but she'd rather cut out her own tongue with a rusty butter knife than say so.

How had she gotten here, anyway? She'd been looking through the binoculars one minute, and the next she was all but flying across the lawn, with no clear idea what she'd say to Joe when she cornered him. Definitely without remembering that she was rapidly turning into Hive Central.

She still didn't know what to say. She could only react. To his dimpled smile. His laughing, mocking eyes. The way he lounged against the kitchen counter, his bare legs crossed at the ankles, his body one tall, dark occasion of sin. Nothing at all like the shirt-sleeved, smiling "J. P. O'Malley" she'd seen posed on the cover of *Newsweek*.

She'd burned her copy. Then gone out and bought another one. Right now it was hidden in her bottom drawer, along with the stuffed penguin he'd won for her at a local carnival, some photographs of them at the beach and a few other things she really ought to toss in the garbage.

"I'm having an allergic reaction," she answered at last. "And, 'y the way, I hate you," she said feelingly. "I really, really, *really* hate you."

"Which probably means I won't be welcome at the wedding next Saturday? Too bad, as I've already got my invitation and responded in the affirmative. I chose the beef dish, in case you're wondering. You know how I never could stand fish. Is it an open bar? Probably. God, Maddy, you're cute when you're swollen, do you know that?"

That did it. Maddy stumbled toward a chair sitting smack in the middle of the room, and sat down on it. Certainly not a good move, but much preferred to the alternative, which was to fall down.

"I cannot 'elieve my very own grandmother could *do* this to me," she said to no one in particular. "Why would she do this to me?"

"That would be Almira, right?" Joe said, locating and opening the bread loaf. "Nice lady. And very concerned for you, you know."

"Concerned? Ha! Allie just likes to 'eddle— *'eddle*. Oh hell, you know what I 'ean." She concentrated on controlling her numb upper lip. It was probably the same size as her nose by now. "Meddle," she pronounced carefully. "And she seems to like Matt so much…and I *thought* she liked me…."

"She says you're unhappy," Joe said, opening the peanut butter jar. There wasn't much sense in trying to pretend Almira Chandler hadn't help set up this entire plot. It didn't have enough twists to make such a defense plausible. So, as he'd stopped lying, he figured he'd go back ten, and punt with the pea-nut butter and jelly.

"She had no 'iness—*business*—telling you that. B-because I'm not unhappy. I'm deliriously happy. *Ecstatic,* even!"

"Uh-huh. Careful, or your nose will start grow-ing. You've got a hive on the tip of it already, you know. Is it okay if we just have peanut butter? I can't seem to locate the jelly."

"Eighteen months," Maddy mumbled under her breath as she reflexively rubbed at the tip of her nose. "Eighteen months of getting myself 'ack to-gether, getting myself on my feet..."

"I'll take that as a yes," Joe said, enjoying him-self very much. After all, those hadn't just been Maddy's eighteen months; they had been his as well. And he hadn't enjoyed too damn many of them, thanks to her.

Poor baby. She really did look like she wanted to crawl out of her bumpy, reddened skin. "Would you like a side of calamine lotion with that?"

Maddy suddenly realized she was going about this all wrong. Using every bit of strength she had, she sat back in her chair and looked up at Joe. "Con-gratulations are in order, I suppose," she said coldly, pronouncing every word with care. "You and Loony Larry seem to have hit the jackpot after all."

Joe's one-sided grin made her want to jump up and pop him one in the nose.

"You always had such a flair for the understate-ment, Mad. Yeah, Larry and I got lucky. Hard work, genius, the guts to go for the brass ring—they had nothing to do with it. Just dumb luck, that's all.

Enough monkeys, working at enough keyboards, or however that goes, probably could have done the same thing.''

''That's not what I meant,'' Maddy said, mentally biting her tongue before she could tell him not to call her Mad. She'd die before she'd tell him that, before she'd say anything else he could use against her. Wasn't it enough that he was using her own grandmother against her? The Harris house against her? His handsome, smiling face and well-remembered body against her?

Did she want his well-remembered body against her?

No, no, she couldn't think that way, wouldn't think that way. Joe was the past, long gone and supposedly forgotten. She refused to think about the hives.

Besides, Matt was her future. Kind, sweet, undemanding Matt. Theirs would be a safe, comfortable marriage, the two of them content with their mutual interests, a desire to settle down, to start a family. Matt wanted children; Maddy wanted children. And they genuinely liked each other. What was so wrong with that?

''No, of course that's not what you meant,'' Joe was saying, bringing Maddy back to attention as she tried, rather vainly, to picture Matt's face in her mind's eye. ''You're happy for me, I'm sure of that. It's just a shame you couldn't have been along for the ride, as it was a lot of fun. I guess you were too busy here in your safe cocoon, finding yourself a nice, safe guy to marry. Banker, right?''

Maddy had a quick vision of her grandmother standing in the center of a huge pot as she, Maddy, lit a fire under it. "Matt is a b-banker, yes. And we're very, very happy."

"Except that I bought *your* house out from under you?"

Now Joe stood beside her grandmother in the pot, carrots and celery floating around him, an onion in his mouth. She'd boil them into a stew. *Les Ragoût de Traîtres.* Traitor Stew. She might serve them over rice.

"I overreacted," she said, dismissing the lovely mental picture. "Somebody b-bought the Harris house just as we were about to make a b-bid, yes. And now I know it was you. Now I know it was Allie who tipped you off. I mean, it doesn't take a rocket scientist to see her fingerprints all over this one. So, yes, I'm...*marginally* upset about that."

"Marginally upset." He handed her a peanut butter sandwich on a paper plate, and she took it—why, she'd never know. "I'd hate to see you really mad, Mad. Do you want something to drink? I've got some cans of soda in the fridge. Sarsaparilla, your favorite."

Sarsaparilla. How he'd made fun of her when she'd told him about that. How she had adored him for scouring all the grocery stores around the university, until he found some for her. And then she'd kissed him, and hugged him, and they'd sort of just *fallen* onto the couch....

"Thank you, no," she said, her molars all but stuck together with peanut butter. Then she faced facts. She needed something to drink before she choked. "I guess I'd b-better have a glass of water, if that's all right?" Lord, was her mouth closed? Her top lip was so huge and rubbery-feeling, she really couldn't tell.

She'd planned never to see Joe O'Malley again. At least not unless it was on her own terms. When he was down, downer and down. When she could lift him up again.

Then he'd gone and made a success of himself, so that he didn't need her at all. He'd probably made a success of himself just to spite her.

Still, here she was, and here he was, and here the hives were, screwing up what could have been a pretty good confrontation. But how do you verbally beat up a guy, call him the bastard that he was, when you couldn't even get your mouth to close enough to form proper-sounding *B*'s?

How could she be sitting in Joe's kitchen—*her* kitchen, damn it!—choking down a peanut butter sandwich and talking as if discussing Allie's duplicity and his arrival on the scene were no more earth-shaking than shared comments on the weather? *Do you think it will rain? Hot enough for you? What are you doing back in my life, uninvited, living next door and offering me sarsaparilla soda?*

As if he could read her thoughts, and he'd had a lot of practice, Joe said, "Amazing, isn't it, Maddy? We've been in this kitchen together for about five minutes, and we're not in each other's arms or killing each other. Who would have thunk it?"

Sudden tears pricked at Maddy's eyes. "Why are you here, Joe? I know what this house cost, and that's a little much just to prove how well you've done, just so you could rub my nose in it, isn't it?" That last bit came out as "sud my oze in it," but she wasn't about to repeat herself.

"Rub your nose in it? Me?" Joe, pretty confident of his translation of that last statement, turned back to the kitchen counter, so that Maddy couldn't see his eyes. She'd always been way too good at reading his eyes. That was how she'd known about the company, he was sure of it, how she'd known to ask those damning questions five minutes before he could marry her, then tell her what he'd done, when it was too late to change the fact that they were married.

Okay, so he'd been sneaky. Underhanded, even. But he'd known, just *known* that she wouldn't go along with his plans unless both the plans and the marriage were already accomplished facts. She'd certainly made that much plain to him a few weeks earlier, when she'd offered him her trust fund and he'd stormed out of her apartment, staying away for two entire days. Any longer, and he would have probably died from missing her.

As he'd been dead these past eighteen months, without her. And, according to Almira Chandler, Maddy hadn't been doing much better. She'd only done her damnedest to give that impression to anyone who hadn't known her and loved her since she was in diapers.

With one cheek stuffed full of peanut butter and fresh bread, he turned to Maddy once more. "Do you really believe I'm the sort of person who would plunk down a small fortune and move in next door to you a week before your wedding, just to drive you nuts?" He swallowed the lump of sandwich, thanking God the peanut butter didn't stick in his throat, just as his next words were sitting there, ready to do the same. "And what if I did? If you don't love me, if you love this Garvey guy, what difference would it make to you?''

He took a short, calming breath, and let her have the rest of it, all of it. Everything he'd wanted to say to her for eighteen months.

''Would I do that? Just to, as you said, rub your nose in the fact—*fact,* Maddy, not dream—that I'd been right, that my ideas did have merit, were worth taking a chance on. Were worth *you* taking a chance on…if you'd really loved me. Damn straight I would!''

Maddy stood up slowly, looked Joe full in the face. Pronounced every word carefully. ''I loved you, Joe,'' she said quietly. ''But you didn't trust me. Not enough to tell me the truth, that's for sure. You were just going to marry me, then blithely mention that, oh, yeah, I just sank every penny I have into a new business that could fall flat on its face, hope you don't mind. You didn't trust *me.*''

Now Joe felt his temper rising, the temper he had thought had cooled long ago, to be replaced by the damning knowledge that, if he were to become rich beyond his dreams—and he had—he would never be happy, complete, without Maddy by his side. He had to love her. If he didn't, he was just plain nuts to be putting himself back into a position where she could cut his knees, and heart, right out from underneath him.

And still, he couldn't help himself. He couldn't keep his big mouth shut, even though he knew Maddy was at least partially right. They were both partially right, and that was the problem. Because they were also both partially wrong.

''I didn't trust *you?* Oh, Mad, you sure have a

warped memory. You didn't trust *me*. But you did trust your trust fund, didn't you? If it had been up to you, we'd be living in that mansion over there, with me working for your brother and slowly suffocating. And all the while living on your trust fund. What was it you said? Oh, yeah, something about me *playing* with my *little idea* on weekends. It would have been easier if you'd treated me like a pet cat, and just had me neutered."

"That's not fair!" Maddy exploded, giving the chair a push, only vaguely surprised when it toppled onto the floor with a small crash. "I offered you my trust fund, Joe, my home. You wouldn't take either of them. And b-besides, you didn't *have* to take a job with Ryan, it was just a suggestion."

"Well, excuse me, but in the words of oppressed men everywhere—*hah!* You all but had me in some office, figuring out the price of yard goods. I'm a software designer, Maddy, not a guy who wants to live off his wife, play golf and slowly drink himself to death."

"That's it, Joe," Maddy exploded. "Twist everything around, forget about how you planned to figure *me* into this equation you'd worked out in your mind. You wanted me to be the little woman b-behind the man, living in some third-floor walkup and trying to figure out another way to cook hamburger—all while you and Larry played at b-becoming the next B-Bill Gates. You didn't want a wife, Joe. You wanted a...a..."

She stopped dead, something he'd said repeating itself inside her head, driving out any other thoughts. "What do you mean, had you *neutered?* Are you actually standing there, saying that I wanted to rob you of your *manhood?* That's not only unfair, it's ridiculous!''

Joe opened his mouth to lash out at her again, then belatedly reined in his temper, let his sense of humor rescue him from what would just turn into a pointless argument, the sort they'd had eighteen months ago. ''So, Mad, do you still love me? I mean, I'd hate to think I bought this house just to drive you nuts.''

''*Ooooh!* How I hate you, Joe O'Malley. How I hate, hate, *hate* you!''

He took a single step toward her. ''And you're being redundant, Maddy. Tell me, in an argument isn't the first person who becomes redundant the first person to have run out of logical points?''

''No, you miserable, rotten...the first person to take a swing at the other guy in an argument is the first one to have run out of logical points. And I'd be happy to run out of them, just so I could pop you one in the nose!''

''Hey, Mr. O'Malley, where do you want us to put your—'' Chad stopped just inside the kitchen, looked at Joe, looked at Maddy. ''Smoke and fire. Right. I forgot. I'll just have Butch put the desk where he wants, okay, and get back to you. Sorry about that.''

Joe waited until the workman was gone, then stabbed his fingers through his hair, still too long but definitely with a better cut. He looked at Maddy, looked straight past the hives, and saw the girl he'd met two years ago behind the glaring eyes of this near stranger who looked, hives, ponytail and all, so very grown up, so different from the girl he'd known. So different from the girl who'd left him standing at the altar, or nearly so, and run home, run away from him. Taken his heart with her.

"I still love you, Maddy," he said, his voice barely above a whisper. "Is it really too late for us? Have I left it too late?"

Maddy felt as if she had swallowed broken glass, the shards having popped whatever balloon of indignation she might have had inside her. "I'm getting married next Saturday, Joe. What do you think?"

"I think I may have left it too late," he admitted, taking a single step in her direction. "I think I should never have let you go in the first place."

The feeling was beginning to come back into her upper lip as the antihistamine belatedly kicked in. All the better to yell at Joe O'Malley, Maddy thought meanly. "I left you," she said, suddenly realizing that a single tear had run down her cheek, but she refused to wipe it away. "You *made* me leave you. It doesn't matter that you're successful now, Joe, just as it didn't matter that you weren't successful eighteen months ago. Don't you understand yet? It was that you wouldn't bend, not even an inch. You wouldn't take the money I offered, you wouldn't even tell me what you were doing because you knew I'd hate it. You just wanted me to give, and give, and give...."

"*Give?* Maddy, Maddy, Maddy, how many times do I have to tell you that I didn't want your money," Joe said, deliberately misunderstanding as he took another step forward, reaching into his back pocket for his handkerchief, which he could use as an excuse to touch her, be close to her.

And maybe so he wouldn't shake her, for having

grown so much, gained so much logic, and so many weapons to use against him, to make him see himself as he didn't want to be seen. As a selfish jerk with more pride than brains...

"No, you didn't. And you didn't want *me* to have it, either. You wanted to jump out of a plane without a parachute and take me with you. It never occurred to you that *I* had a life before I met you, that *I* might not be equipped, practically or emotionally, to find the joy you thought there would be in poverty."

"Money," Joe bit out, shaking his head. "It always comes back to that, doesn't it?"

"Doesn't it, Joe? Tell me, would you be here at all if your idea had fallen flat? If you couldn't come here in that sports car I saw out front, and plunk down the money for this house? If you'd loved me, *really* loved me, wouldn't you have come after me when I first flew home from Las Vegas? I waited, Joe. I waited, and you didn't come. You're only here now to hurt me, as I hurt you eighteen months ago. Admit it to me, Joe, even if you can't admit it to yourself."

He was silent for long moments. "You've grown up," he said at last.

"I had no choice, Joe. One of us had to. Enjoy your new house, and stay out of my life," she said, then whirled on her heels and walked toward the front door, her head held high.

Until Joe's words stopped her.

"Does your fiancé know about me, Maddy?"

She closed her eyes, willed her chin not to wobble. "No, Joe," she admitted quietly. "He doesn't. Only Allie and my sister and brother. No one else. Which is why I know my meddling grandmother brought you here, because Jessie was as surprised as I was, and Ryan is too honest and upright to even think of something so nasty.''

''But Mrs. Chandler isn't that honest and upright?''

His voice came from directly behind her, and she flinched as he put his hands on her shoulders.

''My grandmother lives by her own rules, and never knows when to back off,'' Maddy said, ducking out from beneath Joe's hands, his warm touch. His so inflaming touch.

''I like your grandmother.''

That did it. Maddy whirled around, gave him a push with both hands. ''Good, then you marry *her*. *I'm* marrying Matthew Garvey.''

''Are you, Maddy? Are you really? You wanted this house. I got it for you. I can get you anything you want, with the possible exception of the moon, but I hear it's nothing but rocks anyway. I can give you everything you wanted me to give you eighteen months ago.''

To her complete surprise, but not to Joe's, who had known he was pushing her too far the moment he opened his mouth, Maddy slapped him hard across the cheek, and ran out of the house.

''Stupid, O'Malley,'' Joe said, punching the wall. ''Stupid, stupid, *stupid!*''

Chapter Four

"**S**o, is it safe to come out now?" Almira Chandler asked her granddaughter as she marginally opened her bedroom door and let Jessie slip inside.

Maddy had stomped back into the house a half hour earlier, the fading hives still standing out stark white in her otherwise tear-reddened face, waving her hands and tightly warning her grandmother: "*Don't*...talk to me!"

"I think so," Jessie answered now, sitting down on her grandmother's favorite chair. "She's downstairs, in the family kitchen, whipping up a cake or something. Whatever it is, she isn't using the electric mixer, and I sort of feel sorry for the spoon she is using. Congratulations, Allie. You really did it this time."

Almira patted the front of her dress as she turned, admiring her reflection in the mirror. "Yes, I did, didn't I. Sometimes I even amaze myself."

Jessie had come to her grandmother's room to scold her. But how did you scold a woman like this?

"You're incorrigible. I don't think it would be a good idea if you were to look quite so pleased with yourself the next time you see Maddy. She's really upset, and I don't blame her one bit."

"Of course she's upset," Almira said, waving Jessie out of the pink-and-white chintz chair, so she could sit down. She inspected her cherry-red fingernails, frowned when she saw a small chip in one nail. "You didn't really think she'd be thrilled, did you, darling? People hardly ever are when you're doing them a favor."

"A favor," Jessie echoed, shaking her head. "Allie, you sicced her old boyfriend—fiancé, whatever you want to call him—on your youngest granddaughter only a few days before her wedding to someone else. You called him, you told him what he should do—I still can't believe you actually got him to buy the Harris house—and now Maddy is going to look across the hedges at Joe O'Malley's house as she walks down the garden steps to marry Matt."

Jessie took one small step back, her words fully sinking into her own head. "You don't really think she's going to marry Matt now, do you, Allie? Why? I thought you liked him."

"I do like him, Jessie. Everyone likes Matt Garvey. What's not to like? You like him, don't you?"

Jessie spread her hands, turned and walked away from her grandmother. "Oh, no. No, no, no. We're not going to go there, Allie." She turned back, glared at Almira. "Are we?" she ended, the question more of a threat.

"Who? Me? Of course not, darling. I don't meddle, you know that."

"You don't—you don't meddle? Oh, that's a riot, Allie, a real riot. Okay, what *do* you call what you've done to my poor baby sister?"

Almira twisted the two carat diamond on the third finger of her left hand, straightening it on her finger. "I call it common sense, my dear. And do you know what? If I were all plump and gray-haired and smelled like fresh-baked gingerbread, you'd just say I was being a silly, sentimental old matchmaker. Why, you'd probably think I was cute as a button. Dear old Gran. Matchmaking again. Isn't that sweet?"

She ran her hands down each side of her trim waist and hips as she stood up once more, patted her upswept hair. "Perhaps I should have let myself go to seed. I'd certainly find more sympathy from my ungrateful family."

Jessie stared at her grandmother, her mouth slightly open as she listened to this nonsense. "You're evil, do you know that, Allie? You're positively *evil*."

Almira smiled, patted Jessie's cheek. "Flattery will get you nowhere, darling. Now, let's go see Maddy, all right? Last thing the girl needs right now is to be abandoned by those who love her."

"Abandoned? You threw her to the wolves," Jessie said, chasing after Almira, who could probably outpower-walk most of the citizens of Allentown.

"Oh, don't be so dramatic, Jessie, it isn't like you. It was just one wolf," Almira said as she headed down the wide sweep of stairs. "And I've given her a choice, that's all. You know the state

Maddy was in when she came back to us eighteen months ago. No closure, no real settlement in her mind. And don't forget the hives. You know, rather like the ones she's wearing so badly today.''

"Joseph O'Malley brought on those hives, Allie," Jessie reasoned. "She hasn't had them since a few weeks after she came home, not until today. Now both the hives and the house are on your head. I hope you're happy.''

"Your sister's shattered *nerves* are what brought on the hives, Jessie. Try to concentrate. It's Maddy's diving into all those courses in domestic...domestic whatevers. Picking out Joe O'Malley's exact opposite for her groom. If she were completely sure she's doing the right thing, her nerves shouldn't upset her enough to have her covered in splotches, now should it? Besides, I'm not saying she's wrong, exactly, I'm just saying that she needs to see the two of them stacked up against each other. Sort of weigh them, sort out her own feelings.''

"Inspect their teeth, their bank balances? *Sleep* with both of them?'' Jessie said as they walked back through the house, heading for the kitchen. "That is what you're thinking, isn't it, Allie? I know you. I've seen the books you read.''

Almira stopped dead, ten feet in front of the kitchen door, and turned to hold a finger just beneath Jessie's nose. "Now you listen to me, little girl. I read romance novels. *Love stories*. One man, one woman, true love triumphing over each and every obstacle. I do *not* read about or advocate sleeping with two men at the same time, comparing them like...like automobiles I might be taking out for some sort of test drive. Shame on you for even thinking such a thing.''

"Yes, Allie," Jessie said, bowing her head. "I'm sorry. I guess I must have gotten carried away. Forgive me?"

Almira pulled her taller granddaughter down and kissed her cheek. "Of course I forgive you." Then she whispered in Jessie's ear, "Although, it *could* be interesting...."

"Allie!" Jessie exclaimed, straightening, knowing her cheeks were turning a bright, embarrassed red.

"And, my dear, if it helps you to understand what I'm doing, I have it on good authority that your sister and Matt have *never*—"

"*Allie!*"

Inside the kitchen, sitting on a high stool, her chin tucked into her hands, Maddy lifted her head at the sound of her sister's voice.

She'd gone straight to the family kitchen upon her return, Mrs. Ballantine right behind her, prudently shooing the cook, Mrs. Hadley, and one of the maids out of the area before leaving Maddy to her own devices.

Those devices had included a lot of slamming of pots and pans, a lot of wrenching open of cabinet doors before flinging them shut with considerable force.

And muttering. There had been a lot of muttering.

"He still loves me. Hah!" she'd grumbled, measuring flour and sugar into a stainless steel bowl.

"*I've* got a warped mind? Double hah! *He's* the one with the warped mind. Listening to Allie. Buying *my* house. Coming here with his grin and his money and…and his *knees,* and acting as if it was no big deal.''

She'd stop mixing the brownie batter, staring off into the distance. "*Boy,* is he lucky we don't keep rat poison in the kitchen. Because I'd be *this* close to…'' She'd shivered, shook her head and began abusing the brownie batter once more. "I wouldn't want to waste good food that way,'' she'd told herself just before she sat down with the bowl, licking batter off the wooden spoon.

He'd looked so good. So very, very good. Just the way she remembered. Just the way he appeared in her dreams—no, her nightmares.

She'd fished a clean spoon out of the drawer, and took another whopping scoop of brownie batter.

And then another.

And another.

She could still see Joe standing outside the wedding chapel, telling her he'd blithely made the most tremendous gamble, a gamble he hadn't planned to tell her about until *after* the ceremony, the sneak.

Not that they'd even have gotten as far as the pavement outside the wedding chapel if he'd told her earlier.

He'd certainly had the opportunity. Several opportunities. They'd been together in the hotel for the entire weekend, laughing, and loving…and answering the phone whenever Loony Larry called, which he did at least three times a day.

Ample time. All the time in the world to talk to her, to ask her, one more time, if it would be all right with her if he junked his very good job, his fairly assured future and bet it all on a pipe dream...while demanding that she live on his earnings and not touch her trust fund.

The rat. The low-down, dirty, *cowardly* rat! Hadn't he believed she'd loved him enough to stick with him through the "better or worse" if she'd known up-front?

No, of course he hadn't.

That was what really, really hurt. Had hurt her every day and night for eighteen long months.

She took another spoonful of brownie batter.

That, and knowing that she had been not in the least equipped to handle anything even remotely close to poverty. For crying out loud, she hadn't even been equipped to handle Middle Class!

She'd looked at the contents of the bowl, winced and then grabbed a clean spatula in order to spread what remained of the batter in a nine-by-eleven pan. The brownies were going to be awful. Just awful. She wasn't going to fit into her wedding gown, if she kept eating batter.

And it was all Joe O'Malley's fault. All of it. The brownies, her weight, her hives.

The rat.

The oven timer dinged now and Maddy pulled oven mitts on her hands and removed the tray of brownies as she allowed her thoughts to come to some sort of conclusion. "So now I make brownies, and can sew curtains, and even know to dust before I vacuum, not that I vacuum. Mrs. Ballantine would strangle me with the cord if I ever got within ten feet of the vacuum cleaner. And for what? So he could go and get rich and not need me anymore? The rat. The low-down, dirty—"

"Talking to herself, Jessie," Almira stage-whispered as the two women walked into the kitchen. "I think that's a good sign, don't you?"

"Why, because she's talking to herself, and not screaming at you?" Jessie asked, walking across the large kitchen to bend over the tray of brownies. "Sort of *short,* aren't they? I mean, they sure do smell good, but they don't look as big and fluffy as usual."

Maddy positioned the pan more carefully on the cooling rack and turned her back on the brownies. "I ate some of the batter," she mumbled, avoiding her sister's eyes.

"Some, Maddy? And I don't think that's very healthy. Aren't there raw eggs in brownie batter? You ought to do what I do, grab a spoon and the vanilla fudge ice cream, and go sit in the gazebo and guzzle."

Maddy looked at her sister's taller, leaner frame. Jessie had all the elegance in the family; Jessie and Ryan both. Maddy was shorter, rounder. Definitely rounder. And if she kept eating brownie batter, soon she'd be a house.

A house. Like the house next door. The house next door that had Joe O'Malley in it. Suddenly she was hungry all over again.

"I eat when I'm upset," she said, glaring at her grandmother. "So sue me."

Almira spoke up. "Yours is a petite, hourglass figure, Maddy, darling. Tiny hands and feet, slim ankles, a waist that would have done any Gibson girl proud. But it's those generous breasts and rounded hips that really attract the men. Why, you even have darling little dimples on your elbows and knees. Men like to think they're all grown up and self-sufficient, but what they really want is a nice, soft cushion to rest their head. Ask Elizabeth Taylor, if you don't believe me.''

"Kill her for me, would you?" Maddy said to Jessie, who was, at that moment, pulling the top of her sundress away from her body enough to gaze down at her size 34B bra and sighing sadly.

"Maybe if we made a pact," Jessie suggested. "We *both* kill her, and then we alibi each other."

"Works for me. I'm pretty handy with a shovel now, and there's all that loose dirt I worked over at the bottom of the rose garden last week. She's small and skinny enough that it wouldn't take much to fold her up and stick her in the ground. Pity she isn't bigger, actually. She could have made great compost.''

"Such ingratitude. And to think, Jessie dear, that I haven't even shown you the breast enhancement brochure I brought home from Dr. Stephens's office last week, after we'd discussed my knee lift. All sorts of options for breasts these days, rather like a Chinese menu. Rounded, perky, upthrust, Dolly Parton. You name it. Although it is the one menu where you'd make a mistake if you took one from Column A and one from Column B. Now, out of my way.''

Almira spread out her arms, signaling for her two now bug-eyed granddaughters to part in front of her like the Red Sea, and walked between them to inspect the brownies for herself. "Oh, stop looking at me as if I had two heads. You two ought to go on the stage," she said, then poked a finger in the center of the uncut brownies. "Smell good, Maddy. Tell me, if I let it slip that I've invited Joe to the wedding and he's accepted, do you think you could get angry enough to bake one of those angel food cakes with the little confetti sprinkles in it? We haven't had one of those in weeks.''

Maddy walked over to the double sink, ran water in the mixing bowl. ''Jessie, would you please tell our grandmother to take a flying leap off the nearest—''

''Oh, stop it, Madeline,'' Allie cut in, searching in a drawer for a knife. Brownies were good. Maddy's from-scratch brownies were wonderful. But warm-from-the-oven brownies, Almira had found since her youngest granddaughter had gone domestic on them, were as near to an occasion of sin she'd been in ten long years. ''I did it for the best.''

''The *best! Whose* best? Jessie, ask our grandmother *whose* best she did this for, will you, please? Certainly it couldn't have been *mine.*'' Maddy picked up the water-filled mixing bowl and whirled to face her grandmother across the wide, chopping block table in the center of the huge kitchen. ''And then tell her to duck!''

Jessie fought the impulse to hide under the table, out of the line of fire. ''Now, Maddy, remember what happened the day you turned the garden hose on Ryan, and then found out it was Allie and not him who had been practicing chipping on that newly planted bit of lawn? Remember? She showed up around the corner not a minute after you'd nearly drowned Ryan, the nine iron still in her hand. You know you always regret it when you give in to your temper. Especially when you *hate* apologizing to anyone.''

''That's true enough, on all counts,'' Almira said,

calmly slicing herself a two-inch square wedge of warm brownie and placing it on a piece of antique Beleek china she'd retrieved from the overhead, glass-doored cupboard. "And, as Mrs. Hadley would have your head if you messed up her kitchen, you probably should rethink weapons, at the very least."

Maddy put down the bowl and pressed both hands to her head. "Insane. I'm going insane. I'm surprised I've held on to my sanity this long."

"Hello? Anybody home? Maddy?"

Maddy's head jerked up at the sound of Matthew Garvey's voice. "Oh, God, no. Not now, not now."

"I'll head him off at the pass, give you some time to collect your thoughts," Jessie offered. "And to wash that smear of chocolate off your cheek. And, hey, at least the hives are gone. There is that, right?"

But it was too late. Mrs. Ballantine, who would probably swear on a stack of bibles that she hadn't directed Matt to the kitchens, was probably in the main drawing room right now, doing her best to giggle into her sleeve—not that anyone had ever actually *seen* the woman laugh.

Matthew strode into the kitchen, his white dress shirt open at the neck, his tie missing, looking like a man who had left work early and didn't feel the least bit guilty about playing hooky.

"Ah, here you are, all my favorite ladies in the same place. And do I smell freshly baked brownies?" he asked, walking across the kitchen in his long-legged style to plant a kiss on Maddy's cheek. "Yes, definitely brownies. And they taste good, too."

Matthew Garvey had been a part of the Chandler household for the past three years, ever since Ryan had brought his new friend home after a game of golf at the local country club.

And Matt was definitely the country club, golf slacks and knit shirt kind of guy. The kind of guy who always looked at home in his clothes, whether in the boardroom or on the golf course. He was, Maddy always thought, so "together," so wonderfully self-assured. And so very, very safe.

Tall, leanly handsome, well-tanned. Hair as black as coal, contrasting well with his bright blue eyes. A social pedigree as long as his long legs. And nice. Matthew Garvey was nice; one of the good guys.

And very safe.

Matt was the scion of Richard Garvey, founder of the local, privately held Garvey Bank, and he hadn't been handed a single favor by that father. He'd gotten his degree, started at the bank as a teller, and worked his way up over the past ten years. Now, with his father in semiretirement, he was president of the bank at the age of thirty-six.

Handsome indeed, and handsome was as handsome did, so the saying went. He was not at all volatile. He was, instead, gentlemanly. Old enough to want children, gracious enough to be willing to wait until after the wedding to make demands on Maddy and sane enough to know that mad, passionate love usually doesn't last.

All in all, the perfect arrangement.

All in all, the perfect groom.

All in all…safe.

"Hello, Matt," Almira said as Maddy quickly reached for a paper towel and ran it under the water before scrubbing at the splotch of batter on her cheek. "Did you see the moving trucks next door as you drove up?"

Maddy wondered how much pressure clenched teeth could take before they cracked. "Not now, Allie," she warned from between those clenched teeth, even as she smiled and slid her hand through the crook of Matt's elbow. "You've just *got* to come see what Great-Aunt Harriet sent us, Matt. Come on, I'll show you, and maybe you can help me figure out where we can hide it."

He resisted her attempt to drag him out of the kitchen. "Just a minute, Maddy, okay? No, Almira, I didn't notice the moving van. So, knowing you, I suppose you already know the new owner's name, vital statistics and whether or not they own a grand piano?"

"Oh, God, here we go," Maddy all but groaned, looking to her sister for help.

Jessie, knowing how her grandmother could string out a story for best effect, and how Maddy would react, quickly stepped in. "It's not a they, Matt, it's a him. One owner. His name is Joseph O'Malley. I believe he's from the Philadelphia area. He does something with computers, or software, or something like that."

There. She'd gotten it all out, quick and clean. All except for the fact that eighteen months ago, Maddy had been about to marry that same Joseph O'Malley. But that could wait, right?

"O'Malley?" Matt frowned, repeating the name. "O'Malley. Sofware." Then he looked straight at Almira. "Could that be J. P. O'Malley, the software genius? No, of course not."

Almira tried to make hers an innocent question, and succeeded in fooling one out of three of her listeners. "Why of course not, Matt? He wouldn't be the first Philadelphia businessman to have purchased a summer home here in Allentown. I see nothing out of the usual in it."

"Summer home, Allie?" Maddy felt as if she were strangling—or maybe she just wanted to strangle her grandmother. "You can't possibly call the Harris house a summer home. It has seven bedrooms, for crying out loud!"

"All the better to entertain, my dear," Almira countered, much like the Big Bad Wolf as he flashed his teeth at Little Red Riding Hood. "And, yes, Matt. It definitely is J. P. O'Malley. But he's already asked me to call him Joe. Such a nice, polite young man."

"That's it, I'm outta here," Maddy said, flinging the balled-up paper towel in the general direction of the garbage can and heading for the hallway.

"Be with you in a minute, Maddy," Matt called after her, wondering what was bothering her, as she was clearly upset. Probably she didn't want to talk about J. P. O'Malley because he'd bought the Harris house out from under them. That was understandable. "And, hey, Maddy, didn't O'Malley graduate from Penn like you? He's called a boy genius, so he probably isn't more than two or three years older than you. Did you ever meet him?"

Maddy stopped at the swinging door that led from the kitchen, her shoulders hunched defensively, her back still turned to Matt. "I may have, once or twice," she lied, wondering, just for an instant, why she was lying to the man.

Then she remembered why she'd lied, why she'd never told Matt about Joe, not when she'd first come home, not when they'd begun to date, not even after he'd slipped the diamond circlet on her left hand.

She hadn't told him *because it still hurt.* It still hurt way down deep inside of her. Joe, and the memory of him, were still open wounds, just barely beginning to scab over, and still far from healed. Talking about Joe, with Jessie, with Allie, with her own doctor, with *anybody,* was still just too painful.

"You're staying for dinner, aren't you, Matt?" she asked, daring to turn around, daring her betraying tears not to fall. "I'll just go up to my kitchen and get the leg of lamb out of the fridge." Maybe take another antihistamine, as her upper lip was beginning to tingle ominously again.

When she had gone, Matt accepted a plate holding a wedge of brownie from Almira. "I knew losing the house upset Maddy, but I guess I didn't realize just how much she'd wanted it. She said she'd be perfectly happy living here for a while longer, while we looked for another house," he said, looking at Jessie.

"Bridal nerves," Jessie lied quickly, feeling very protective of her sister, protective of Matt as well. "This morning I found her crying over the favors for the guests that had just been delivered, telling me they were just too pretty for words. She'll be fine."

"She'll be ducky," Almira agreed, patting Matt's cheek as she headed out of the kitchen. "Just ducky. Everything will be perfect, I promise."

Chapter Five

Joe lay back on the brand-new, soft chaise longue beside his brand-new pool, his legs crossed at the ankles, his hands behind his head. It was nine o'clock in the morning, and the sun was shining, he'd already had breakfast, Maddy was next door—hating his guts—and life was good.

Hopefully, soon to get better.

He'd been in residence for less than twenty-four hours, and already he felt very much at home.

He'd gone out for dinner the previous evening, as the limited staff he'd hired hadn't yet arrived, and slept in his king-size bed after locating a set of deep green sheets from the bottom of one of the packing boxes.

This morning, after drinking orange juice direct from the container, he'd gone on a hunt for a pair of swimming trunks, then gone out to the pool to swim a dozen laps.

Now here he was, lazing in the sun, beads of water still clinging to him, a pair of designer sunglasses shading his eyes and, in general, feeling pretty damn smug.

He could really get used to this. Life in the countryside, with birds chirping in the trees, flowers all around. So very different from the small Philadelphia row house he'd grown up in, light years away from his Philly condo that had all the bells and whistles, but not a single chirping bird outside his bedroom window.

Pigeons, he'd decided, didn't count.

Such a long trip, all the way from South Philly to the classiest Allentown suburbs. His dad, who had taken a hike when he was two and never contacted him again until after the *Newsweek* cover—to hit him up for a loan—would never see this part of Joe's life.

His mother, who had died so suddenly three days after his nineteenth birthday, never could, even though Joe wished her here with all his heart.

He'd worked for his mother, worked every day. In school. In odd jobs. Soaking up knowledge like a sponge, because his mother promised him that knowledge was his way out, his way ''up.'' And he'd earned his way. He'd unloaded fruit and vegetable trucks at Sal's Grocery, delivered newspapers every morning. He had even run numbers for Jimmy Jumbo Ears Moscotti for about two weeks, until his mother had found out.

Fifteen, and big for his age, his petite mother had jumped into the air in order to slap his face, tell him she hadn't been scrubbing other people's toilets for twenty years so that her only child could go flush himself down one of them. His mother had always had a way with words....

So he'd returned to his studies with a new determination; graduated top of his class of six hundred, earned a full scholarship to the University of Pennsylvania. His mother had lived to see his name on the dean's list, but not to see him graduate.

What a life. What mixed memories.

And now this.

He'd learned a lot in his twenty-seven years, most of it from his mother, plenty of it from his teachers and the rest from the gritty streets of South Philly. But he'd never quite gotten over the stigma of being poor in a world that values material wealth.

So now he had it. All the money his hard work could bring him. More money than he'd expected or knew what to do with, truthfully. Enough money to tell himself that he was just as good as anyone else, maybe even better than some, and that, damn it, he deserved some happiness in his personal life.

Except that happiness still eluded him, had left him standing on the Strip in Vegas with fifty bucks in his pocket; had made him feel, yet again, what it was like to be the poor boy from South Philly, the guy with more dreams than brains. The guy with only a shadowy vision of a better future, and still struggling with his absent father's legacy of failure.

Joe had told himself over and over, all through the years, that he was his mother's son, not his father's image. He'd told himself that until he'd actually begun to believe it.

He'd told himself that even as he'd gone back to the hotel room to find Maddy's suitcases gone.

And then, mad at Maddy, mad at his dad, mad at the world, he'd gone off to prove it.

The sharp spray of cold water hit his chest and face. "What in *hell*...?" He pulled off his sunglasses, squinted up at the tall form standing over him.

"It's a warm morning. I thought you could use some cooling off."

Joe rubbed a hand across his drenched face, sluicing off water, and blinked several times. Felt the quick anger invade him, just as quickly tamped it down. He knew this wasn't going to be easy. Nothing in his life had been easy. "Let me take a wild shot at this one. You'd be the fiancé?"

"Wrong. I'd be the brother," the sun-shadowed image corrected, redirecting the hose nozzle before turning off the spray. "And you'd be the louse, right?"

"News travels fast around here," Joe said, standing up to wipe his hands on the towel he'd snatched from a nearby table. He held out his right hand. "Joe O'Malley, louse, at your service. Pleased to meet you, Ryan Chandler. And thanks for only pelting me with water, and not beating me with the hose while you were at it. I'd expected a punch in the mouth, to tell you the truth. Maddy always told me you were a very protective older brother."

"That wasn't for Maddy," Ryan said, ignoring Joe's hand. "That was for me. You've already screwed up Maddy's life once. Now you seem to be back, trying to do it again, God only knows why. I suppose it wouldn't help if I were to ask you to go away, leave my sister alone? I could threaten to beat you black and blue, too, if you really want me to.

Only I'd have to make it all gut shots. If Maddy saw you with a black eye, she'd probably feel sorry for you."

Joe withdrew his hand, pretended to wipe something from his chest. He looked at Ryan Chandler, man of the house, head of the business, and one tall, muscular-looking son of a gun. Hair as black as Maddy's, eyes just as green. Now that the sun wasn't half-blinding him, even with Chandler's longer face, squarer jaw, Joe would have been able to pick Maddy's protective big brother out of a crowd.

He shook his head. "Sorry, no. It wouldn't help if you flattened me. I'd still stick around. But my gut most gratefully thanks you. I'm here to stay, Mr. Chandler, or at least for the duration—until after the wedding. If there is a wedding. It's just another of my wild, reckless gambles, as Maddy would tell you."

Ryan lifted one expressive eyebrow. "Really. You're betting over a million dollars that Maddy would take one look at you and toss Matt into the nearest garbage can? That's one damn healthy ego you've got, O'Malley."

"Yeah," Joe said, smiling his best *I'm a nasty little rascal, but please love me anyway* smile. It had always worked to get a free doughnut out of Mrs. George at the South Street Bakery, but he didn't have much hope that it would help him now. "Sometimes I have to beat this ego of mine down with a stick. And you're underestimating the bargaining power of the Harris Realtor. By about a million. But it will be worth it, every penny, if I can stop Maddy from making the second biggest mistake in her life.''

Joe watched as a small tic began in Ryan Chandler's tanned left cheek. ''I take it all back, O'Malley. You don't have a big ego. You're *all* ego, top to bottom. Do you really think Maddy's going to go all soft and gooey because you bought this house? You do, don't you?''

''I just want a chance, that's all. A chance to prove to Maddy that I love her, that I still want to marry her. If I can't convince her, this house will be her wedding present. I owe her that much. Twice as much, and more. I doubt I'd be the success I am today if I hadn't been trying so hard to prove her wrong about me.''

The eyebrow lifted again, and Joe thought he saw a quick flash of sympathy in Ryan Chandler's eyes. ''That's pretty pathetic, you know.''

Joe grinned quite naturally, relaxing his guard now that he knew he wasn't going to get punched. ''Damn straight, Ryan, if we can be informal? I'm pathetic, more than pathetic. Desperate is probably an even better word. When Almira got hold of me a month ago, said this was the way to go, I took it, even if, between you and me, it sounded nuts. But I've got to say that it sure got Maddy over here in a hurry. She can hardly ignore me, not when I'm living next door.''

Ryan took the towel from Joe, gave a few quick swipes across the seat of a nearby chair in case it had caught some of the splash, and sat down. He was wearing a suit and tie, as he'd been on his way to the plant when his feet had somehow taken a right turn, leading him to the old Harris house. Now the O'Malley house.

"You really love her?" he asked, looking straight at Joe, trying to look straight through him to his motives. "Or do you just hate losing?"

Joe grimaced as he sat down as well. "I'm not a good loser, I'll grant you that. But if I thought Maddy was happy with this Matthew Garvey guy, I'd back off. Almira doesn't seem to think so. She convinced me—that wasn't hard—and, well, here I am."

"Yes, my grandmother. That's the second time you've mentioned her. Maddy isn't speaking to her, not that I blame her. But we did have the greatest leg of lamb and all the trimmings last night, so it's not that bad. Cook never could get the hang of leg of lamb. Always tastes like mutton when she does it."

Joe hadn't understood half of what Ryan Chandler had just said. "Almira, your grandmother...she cooks?"

Ryan slapped his palms against his knees, and stood up. "Allie cooks, all right. She cooks up plots to drive the rest of us insane. But Maddy *really* cooks. When she's happy, when she's sad, when she's mad as hell...she cooks. It would be easier to break your nose for you this morning if I hadn't eaten so well last night."

"Maddy cooks?" This didn't compute for Joe, who could visualize Maddy in a lot of places. The kitchen wasn't one of them. "Are we talking about the same Maddy here?"

Ryan looked down at the man who had broken his baby sister's heart. He really wanted to hate the guy, but he could see how Maddy had fallen in love with him. He was just the sort to intrigue her: handsome, fairly witty—which couldn't have been easy this morning—and with that almost tangible air of adventure about him.

Like a pirate of old, Ryan thought, or some such nonsense, just the sort of exciting creature his sister would fall for, want to mother. And definitely a self-made man, a guy who had come up the hard way, determinedly climbing the ladder to success one difficult rung at a time.

Ryan envied Joe O'Malley that. He'd been handed everything on a silver platter the day he'd been born, and still, at the age of thirty-two, didn't know how to say, "No, thank you," and get out. He wanted to ask O'Malley what it was like to see your dream and go after it.

"You got rich, Maddy went domestic," Ryan admitted now, knowing he was giving Maddy's secrets away. "Domestic, and frugal, and pretty much the perfect hausfrau, if I'd dare to call her that, and I won't. She's even gotten Cook to start clipping coupons before going to the grocery store. Seems you've both made a lot of changes in your lives in eighteen short months. I wonder why...and just who all the changing was for. You might want to think about that, O'Malley. You and Maddy both. See you around."

"Yeah, right," Joe mumbled, Ryan's words echoing in his ears. Knotting in his stomach. Making him doubt himself for the first time in a long time. Kind of like his mom's slap to the cheek all those years ago.

Joe watched Ryan retrace his steps along the

poolside, then let himself out of the six-foot-high cedar fence. He might have said goodbye, but Joe couldn't be sure.

He rubbed a hand across his mouth, shook his head a time or two, then lay back against the chaise.

He'd gotten as rich as he could, worked as hard as he could, so that he could come to Maddy not only as her financial equal, but richer, more successful than the Chandler family.

While she was learning how to be the wife of a struggling dreamer.

"God, what idiots we are," he said, standing up and diving into the pool to cool his heated mind... the mind that had so meanly pointed out that Maddy had gone one step further. She was engaged to be married....

"Ryan's leaving," Jessie said, exhaling in genuine relief. "And he didn't hit him."

"Pity," Almira said as Jessie allowed the curtain to fall back into place. "I'd give Harriet's tea caddy to see Ryan get ruffled, take a poke at someone. Boy's entirely too controlled, you know, like his father. If he can't loosen up a little bit, have some fun, the least he could do is punch someone's lights out."

Jessie eyed her grandmother warily. "So, if I can follow your corkscrewed logic at all, you'll be setting up a match for Ryan and the heavyweight champ next month?" she asked, retreating from the attic window, the best vantage point for seeing into O'Malley's enclosed pool area.

Jessie felt like a fool, eavesdropping on their new neighbor, but Allie shouldn't be left alone when she was in one of her meddling moods. It was too dangerous, for all of them. "I'll have to remember to buy him a jump rope and some iodine."

"Oh, I'm much more subtle than that, Jessie," Almira said as they made their way back to the third floor. She stopped in the square foyer just outside the double doors that led to Maddy's apartment. "Except when dealing with Maddy, of course. She never gets the point of subtle. Her I knock over the head, just to get her attention."

"Well, congratulations, Allie, I think you've gotten it," Jessie told her, drawing her grandmother away from the double doors, doors that she was eyeing much too speculatively to suit Jessie. "Come on, it's time you left for your appointment with Francis. Your gray roots will be showing up any day now, you know."

Almira quickly lifted a hand to her hair, withdrew it just as rapidly. "You're only saying that so you can go off to the plant without worrying about what I'm going to do next. But, believe me, I'm out of it now. I set it up. It's up to Maddy and Joe to take it from here. That's the difference between setting up probabilities and meddling, dear."

"And yet I've heard through the household grapevine that you've got some sort of pool going with the staff as to when Maddy and Joe get back together. If that's not meddling, Allie, I don't know what is."

Almira stopped on the wide staircase leading to the first floor, and turned to confront her firstborn granddaughter. "You're trying too hard to be obtuse, dear. I'm not just helping Maddy, and you know it. So why don't you just be a good girl and go to work, and let me handle things here.''

Jessie blinked back sudden tears. "He made his choice, Allie.''

"Uh-huh," Almira said, touching a hand to Jessie's forearm. "And it was a good one, as he chose a Chandler. And just think, he only missed by one. But I've got it all in hand, dear, I've got it all in hand. Now, before you go running off to work, Jessie, why don't you go next door and introduce yourself to our new neighbor, just as your brother and sister have done. Never let it be said that Chandlers don't know the proper etiquette required of longtime residents when someone new comes into the neighborhood.''

Jessie nearly tripped on the last step leading to the huge marble floored foyer of this mansion that had been built just after the first World War, back when craftsmanship was mandatory as well as economical. "Go over there and introduce myself? You've got to be kidding!''

Mrs. Ballantine appeared in the foyer as if conjured out of the mist, holding the beige linen jacket of Jessie's suit as well as her purse and car keys. "Miss Jessie?" she said, her face and eyes blank enough to make her a real contender in any high-stakes poker game.

Jessie took the suit coat automatically, shrugged herself into it. "What…what do I *say* to the man?''

"Nothing much, dear," Almira said. "Just accept his offer to take you out to dinner this evening. Take him to the club, as your guest, feed the poor, suffering man some red meat. That will be more than sufficient.''

"Offer to take me…to take me *out to dinner?* To the club? Aren't Maddy and Matt having dinner there tonight with…oh, wait. Wait just one cotton-picking minute! Are you saying you actually have some sort of *game plan* in effect here? What do I do Thursday—seduce the guy in the gazebo?"

Almira looked at Mrs. Ballantine. Mrs. Ballantine looked at Almira.

"Not bad, not bad," Almira said. "In fact, I wish I'd thought of that one, as the gazebo is just outside Maddy's windows." She looked over at Mrs. Ballantine, just for an instant.

Mrs. Ballantine blinked. Just a blink, nothing more, but Jessie had seen it.

"No! Absolutely not. You said you'd set it all up, Allie, that you're through meddling. How do you keep your lies straight? You tell so many of them. Well, I will *not* be a party to this. Not to *any* of it. You understand? That's my *sister* up there, *scratching,*" she ended, wildly pointing in the direction of the stairs. "Shame on you. Shame on you both!"

"Oh, all right, all right," Almira said, her expression making it clear how sad she was to have this kink thrown into her well-laid Machiavellian plans.

Jessie relaxed. "I'm glad you've finally come to your senses. Both of you," she ended, glaring at Mrs. Ballantine before snatching her purse and keys from the housekeeper. "I was really beginning to worry there for a moment. I'm sorry if I yelled."

"You never yell, darling. You're a lady down to your toes. Sadly." Almira put her hand against Jessie's upper arm and began gently steering her toward the front door. "Besides, I just remembered that I have to drive to Reading with Maddy this afternoon. Something about going straight to the supplier to check on the correct shade of linens for the dining tables. I'm sure we'll be back in time for dinner, but you never know, do you? It would be pointless having you and Joe at the country club if Maddy isn't there.''

Jessie dug in her heels again just as Mrs. Ballantine opened the front door. ''Isn't there? Allie, what are you planning now?''

''Nothing, dear, nothing. You've discovered all my plans and shot them down quite effectively. But it is comforting to know you'll be here to entertain Matt if we are late for some reason. You're such a good hostess. Now, have a good day at work, and please don't detain me any longer. You know how Francis can pout when I'm late.''

The door shut on Jessie's last ''But...but...'' and Almira and Mrs. Ballantine stood there quietly for a moment, saying nothing.

Then they exchanged high fives....

Chapter Six

Joe pushed back the cuff of his blue dress shirt and checked his watch one last time. Six o'clock.

Six o'clock, and no Jessie Chandler.

It would seem that Almira's Grand Plan had hit a snag, because Maddy's older sister was supposed to have picked him up at five-thirty.

Or maybe he had been expected to pick her up? No, that couldn't be. He distinctly remembered—

"Ah, the hell with it," Joe muttered, grabbing his sport coat from the back of the chair and slipping it on. The evening was a bust, he was hungry and he was going to drive around town until he found a restaurant that appealed to his sophisticated palate. "It was a lousy plan anyway."

A passing thought that if he didn't have to be in a sport coat and tie he should change into something more comfortable came and went, as he was willing to bet Maddy had never seen him dressed this way before. It might give her a whole new image of him, if he happened to see her on his way out to find himself some friendly golden arches. If he was in a really haute cuisine mood, he'd spring for a double cheeseburger.

Still, he missed his jeans and sweatshirts. They had been one of the beauties of being a struggling software inventor. Casual dress. Sometimes downright sloppy dress. Making it to the big show hadn't changed his wardrobe all that much, as it seemed that khakis and knit shirts were the uniform of the computer world. Starched shirts, ties and wing tips were about as common in his business as manual typewriters.

He made it halfway down the stairs when he remembered that he'd left his car keys on his bureau. Or maybe on the bathroom floor, when he'd stripped, showered. He really wasn't sure. For a bright man, he felt like his brain had become prone to sudden, unexpected "crashes" ever since that first, bizarre phone call from Almira Chandler.

"I'm falling apart here," he told himself, bounding back up the steps two at a time. "And no wonder I can't find anything. I could put my whole condo in this place and still have room for an eight-lane bowling alley. With snack bar," he ended, stomping down the hallway to the master suite.

He must have been out of his mind to buy this house. This huge, rambling house. This house that cried out for a wife, and a bunch of kids, and a twenty-foot-high Christmas tree in the foyer, with the curved stairway as the backdrop.

There should be Easter Egg hunts on the vast lawn. Birthday parties in the huge breakfast room, intimate dinner parties in the smaller dining room, all-out bashes that took up the entire first floor.

And he could picture all of it. With Maddy by his side, with their kids digging their fingers into their very first birthday cake, or sleeping in their rooms as Mommy and Daddy made an early night of it themselves.

Only he was alone, and if Maddy married this Garvey guy, and he held to his promise to give her this house as a wedding present, he'd never see any of it. Garvey would.

The street kid part of Joe growled low in his throat as he pushed open the door to the bedroom suite and headed for the bureau. Then he stopped cold, looked at the framed, blown-up photograph of him with Maddy on the beach in Atlantic City.

He picked up the photograph, then sat down on the edge of the bed, tracing a finger over Maddy's smiling face. They'd been so happy, so carefree.

So unaware that love never was, never had been, enough.

They'd been so happy, so damn happy. They'd met in a small coffee shop after the university library had closed for the night, sharing the last open table as they'd sipped coffee and munched on nearly day-old doughnuts. Talking until the owner threw them out, walking the streets of University City Philadelphia until the sun came up, startling them both.

They'd hardly been apart that first night. If Joe believed in love at first sight, he would say he'd been in love with Maddy since they'd both tried to sit down at the same small table at the same time.

But he knew that wasn't it. He hadn't fallen in

love with her until he'd realized that he'd been talking about his software ideas for three hours and she hadn't once yawned or moaned or thrown a coffee cup at him.

"Why didn't you tell me to shut up?" he'd asked her.

"Because you seem so happy, talking about your work...and because I can't seem to get enough of your smile," she'd answered with an honesty that staggered him.

That had been the beginning. And if all they'd had was their beginning, that would have been fine. The middle had been great, too, and they'd just about moved in together as he completed his work in the library and she studied for finals. They were together so much that it just seemed silly not to bring clothing to each other's apartments, spend most of their nights together.

Young love, first love, whatever kind of love it had been, it had been great. No arguments, no problems. Just lots of love, lots of laughter, lots of sweet, searing lovemaking, lots of cold pizza for breakfast.

Until, shortly after her last class for the semester, he'd asked her to marry him, and the talk finally turned to their future.

"Oh, Maddy, why couldn't your father have been a plumber, or a carpenter?"

Joe stood up, replaced the photograph and grabbed his keys. That wasn't the answer, he knew. If the two of them had come from more similar circumstances, they still would have differed in many ways.

Ways that made them interesting to each other. Ways that drew them to each other.

Ways that had torn them apart.

But people could learn, couldn't they? They could change? Or did they only learn how to hide their spots better, like a leopard hunkered down in tall grass?

Joe slammed out of the house, sick of thinking, of having his thoughts go round and round in his head until they began to argue with themselves.

Besides, it was too late to back out now. He was here. Maddy was here.

And the wedding was scheduled to take place in exactly one week. If he was going to do more than upset Maddy, make her hate him more than she already believed she did, he'd better start figuring out some way to get back into her good graces. Back into her arms. Back into her life.

Or at least insinuate himself into the Chandler household, where he had his only ally. A nutcase, a hopeless romantic with a mind a combination of Dear Abby and Genghis Khan, but an ally nonetheless.

He'd reached his car before he realized he'd not only lost it, but he'd gone even farther around the bend of mental idiocy than he'd thought possible.

He turned, looked back at his new house. "Keys. I forgot to put the damn house key on my damn key chain."

Joe figured he had two ways to handle this.

He could get in his car, find the nearest fast-food restaurant, chomp down some of his favorite saturated fat and cholesterol...or he could go next door and ask if they happened to have an extra key to his house.

They wouldn't, of course. That was the sort of

thing people did in his old neighborhood. Gave a key to the next-door neighbor "just in case." Just in case someone got locked out. Just in case someone was needed to feed the goldfish while someone was in the hospital or on vacation. Just in case a kid was stranded outside because his mom was late coming home from work on the bus.

Just in case someone's mom hadn't been seen for more than a day and a night and someone decided to take a peek inside and found that mom lying on the floor in the living room, past any neighborly help.

Shaking off that thought, and the memory of the phone call he'd gotten at his dorm from Mrs. Petinsky, Joe cut across the wide sweep of lawn dividing his new house from the Chandler mansion. He vaulted over the white split rail fence and looked down to see that the Chandlers' freshly cut lawn was making a shag rug out of his shiny black shoes, and kept on going.

Maddy was in that house. His life, his future, was in that house. And no matter how pathetic he'd look asking if someone could help him get back into his own house, he was going to go for it. After all, what did he have to lose?

"Dignity. Self-respect. Just small stuff," he muttered to himself as he pressed the doorbell, then bent down to wipe bits of grass off his shoes and cuffs.

Moments later the door was opened by a fairly tall young woman with chin-length brown hair and huge blue eyes. She was a pretty woman, definitely one of the Chandlers. Jessie, he thought the name was.

She looked about as happy to see him as she

might be if he were a door-to-door salesman standing there holding a bunch of brushes in one hand
and a bottle of Super-Dooper Cleaning Fluid in the
other.

"Yes?" she said, still standing half behind the
door. "May I help you?"

She knew who he was. She'd have to, as he'd
seen the outline of three female bodies yesterday,
standing behind a window, spying on him.

But, hey, if she wanted to pretend she didn't rec-
ognize him, he could play along. He was flexible.
Nobody could say he wasn't flexible. Except
Maddy.

"Hi, there, ma'am," he said brightly, putting out
his right hand. "My name is Herb Gattling and I'm
running for United States Representative in your dis-
trict. Hope I can count on your vote this November.
If you want, I can explain my position on automatic
pay raises for Congress every six months. If elected,
I think I'll be all for 'em."

"Joe O'Malley," Jessie responded, trying not to
smile as she took his hand in hers, felt his warm,
dry grip. "I knew I shouldn't try to pretend otherwise. I recognize you from the cover of *Newsweek.*
Hello, and welcome to Allentown. Please come in.
Oh, and I'm Jessie Chandler."

"Jessie of the First Place cup in the Junior Ice
Skating Tournament? Jessie, who got straight A's
all through school, so that her sister could spend her
school days hearing teachers remind her that she
wasn't quite the student her sister had been? Are you
really that Jessie?" Joe ended with a smile as he
stepped into the foyer. "The one who taught her
little sister how to ride her first bike, apply her first

mascara and who, if not quite worshiped by that same little sister, has certainly been put on a pedestal by her. Right?''

"Maddy talks too much," Jessie said, grimacing as she led the way into the larger of the two drawing rooms. "Matt, Joe O'Malley is here," she said, and Joe hesitated only a moment before walking into the room as a tanned man dressed in a casually open-necked white dress shirt and slacks stood up and moved toward him.

"Mr. O'Malley," Matt said, shaking his hand. "Matt Garvey. I'm very pleased to meet you."

You wouldn't be if you knew what I was after, Joe thought, his own handshake also firm, maybe too firm. Hell, a little not so friendly arm wrestling could always be an option. Joe was game.

"Thank you, Mr. Garvey," he said, smiling his most ingratiating smile. "I'm pleased to meet you as well." Then he looked at Jessie Chandler, who seemed to be memorizing the pattern on the Oriental carpet at her feet. "I just came over to use your phone, call a locksmith. It seems as if I've somehow locked myself out. I'm not interrupting anything, am I?''

Jessie shot him a look that seemed a little intense.

"No...oh, no, not at all," Jessie said, seating herself on a dark green couch and motioning for both men to sit down as well. "I was just entertaining Matt while he waits for Maddy, my sister, to come back from an errand." She turned to Matt, smiled weakly. "I'm sure she won't be much longer."

"That's all right, Jessie," Matt said. "We all know Maddy can get sidetracked when she's shopping. It's how I ended up with that electric tie rack last month. Unless I'm keeping you from something…?''

Oh, brother. These people were being so damned polite to each other. Almost as if they were strangers who had just met, which couldn't be possible, because Almira said Matt had been a friend of Ryan Chandler's for about three years. They had to know each other.

So why the stilted politeness? Maybe, Joe considered, they really didn't like each other, and stilted politeness was just another way of verbally slapping each other in the face?

Or maybe they liked each other too much, and stilted politeness was the only thing that kept them from falling into each other's arms.

Now, there was a thought worthy of Almira Chandler. Except that Almira had said no such thing to him, hadn't even hinted at it. Which she would have done, Joe thought, if she'd thought he needed to know.

But would he need to know? Would he even want to try to get Maddy back by pointing out that it was possible her worshiped, perfect sister had a crush on her fiancé, and possibly vice versa?

Nah. He wouldn't use information like that, even if he knew it for certain. Maddy would come back to him because that was how their lives were supposed to be played out, side by side with each other.

As if the thought of her had conjured her, the front door opened and Maddy all but ran through the foyer, calling out as she headed for the drawing room. ''Matt? I'm *so* sorry I'm late. It was like I needed dynamite to get Allie to move, I swear. As if I wanted to spend another minute looking at so much as one more—''

She skidded to a halt just inside the drawing room entrance. "You," she mouthed silently, closing her eyes for the space of two heartbeats. "I'm sorry," she said, smiling in recovery as she continued into the room. "I didn't know we had company. Jessie?"

"This is Mr. O'Malley, Maddy," Jessie supplied helpfully. She shouldn't have wasted her time, because the woman had a pretty face, but she didn't have a liar's face. Not with that tendency to blush that had her cheeks turning a delightful pink. "He's our new next-door neighbor. He's locked himself out."

"Really?" Maddy responded, one eyebrow lifted. She had a much better liar's face, Maddy did, and Joe silently applauded her. "How...nice. Except for the locking yourself out part, of course. I think we actually have a spare key, Jessie, if you want to ask Mrs. Ballantine. Mrs. Harris was always locking herself out. So happy to meet you, Mr. O'Malley."

He extended his hand, but she pretended not to see it, walking straight past him to put her arms out to Matt as he stood up to kiss her proffered cheek. "Hello, darling."

Joe smiled, encouraged, as Jessie went in search of Mrs. Ballantine and the spare key. If Maddy didn't care about him, she wouldn't bother to lie about whether or not she'd ever known him. She would have told this Matt Garvey guy—nice guy, Joe thought, which was a pity, because he was going *down*—all about him and they would have had a huge laugh over how she had once dated the new software king.

But she hadn't told him about her past, their love affair, that fateful trip to Las Vegas. She hadn't told him a single thing about her old lover, her first lover.

Her only lover? If that peck on the cheek was to be believed, yeah.

Interesting. Very interesting. Everything Almira Chandler had told him it would be.

And, speaking of Almira the Plotter, with the energy of a twelve-year-old and the smiling face of a woman born to flirt—and revel in it—she just about bounced into the room.

"Hello, all! Joe, how nice to see you again. Settling in, are you? My, don't you look handsome in that shirt. Matches your eyes. But you probably already know that, you devil, you. In fact, I'll bet you have an entire closet *stuffed* with blue shirts. Matt, Jessie, I've had the most lovely day!"

Everyone had already turned to watch Almira Chandler come into the room, dropping packages in her wake as she crossed the room and collapsed onto one of the couches.

"What a day, children, what a day! I can't believe the *bargains* one can get at those Reading outlet stores. I thought it would be a lark, having Maddy take us there for a peek after we looked at linens, but then she practically had to *drag* me out of those wonderful, wonderful stores. Does anyone here wear a size six?"

"I do, Allie," Jessie said, warily eyeing the packages as she reentered the room and handed Joe a single key on a bright gold key chain. "Why?"

"Oh, good," Almira exclaimed, bouncing back up from the couch with the energy of a long distance runner. She went straight to a pink plastic bag and pulled out the sexiest, most ridiculous looking sheer ivory negligee in the history of sexy lingerie. It even had a matching feather boa.

"Allie..." Jessie said, backing away as her grandmother approached her.

"Oh, stand still, darling," Almira said, winking at the two men as she wound the boa around Jessie's throat.

Jessie inhaled, nearly swallowed a stray feather, and felt herself blushing to the roots of her hair as Almira held the negligee up to her, pulling the sheer material taut over her breasts. "There, boys. What do you think? Not at all bridal, but then, who needs bridal, right? Some things are just for the fun of it."

Joe copped a quick look at Matt Garvey's strained features and thought that the French sure could have used a few strategists like Almira Chandler at Waterloo. "Very nice. Very nice," he said.

"She bought one for herself, too. In hot pink, no less," Maddy said, rolling her eyes. "So? Are we ready to go?"

Joe shook his head, pitying both Maddy and Jessie, who clearly were uncomfortable, each for her own reasons. For himself, he was enjoying himself mightily.

There was a whole lot going on in the Chandler drawing room, several layers and levels of intrigue and misdirection, although it seemed that only he and Almira knew about any of it. What would happen if everyone else were let in on the joke? All the not-so-funny jokes?

"Yes," Matt echoed, coughing into his fist, struggling gentlemanly to find a way out of what could only be a bad situation getting worse. "Very nice, indeed, Almira. You made a good choice. And you're ready to leave, Maddy? Anybody else hungry? I'm starved. Why don't the five of us go out for something to eat?''

''Five of us?'' Almira parroted, looking confused. Then she brightened. ''Oh, no. No, no, no, Matt, thank you anyway. I'm *exhausted,*'' she went on, deliberately drooping her shoulders, just a moment too late to look less than ready for a quick four minute mile in stiletto heels. ''I think I'll just have some soup and a sandwich, and make an early night of it. But you four go on, have a nice time, get to know each other better.''

''Allie, no, I don't think—'' Maddy said quickly.

''Sounds good to me,'' Matt said at the same time, looking toward Joe.

''My...my hair,'' Jessie offered quickly. ''I thought I'd wash—''

''Works for me, too,'' Joe said brightly, pulling the keys to his Mercedes out of his pocket. ''My car's already out of the garage, so we could all go in it. That way somebody can give me directions.''

''But—''

Almira cut Maddy off in midprotest. ''Well, then, that's settled. Good. Have a lovely evening, children. And, Joe? Don't let Matt try to talk you into putting all your money in his bank. Only half of it,'' she said with a wink, then picked up her packages and all but skipped out of the room.

''Miserable, conniving...'' Maddy gritted out almost under her breath, but Joe was standing close and overheard her.

''I love her madly,'' he whispered quietly to her as he took her arm, led her toward the foyer. ''In fact, if you won't marry me, I may ask Almira to elope with me instead."

"I think I already suggested something like that," Maddy countered, pulling her arm free, halting to wait for Matt. "Darling?" she said, slipping her hand around his elbow, holding on to him in a near-death grip. "I've missed you today."

"I've missed you, too, Maddy, but I'm glad you and Almira had such a good time," Matt answered, patting her hand.

Joe fought back the urge to gag. He'd seen more passion in a dog food commercial.

He stayed where he was as Jessie slowly brought up the rear, then held out his arm to her so that she really had no choice but to take it. "I'm sorry I didn't phone to cancel the dinner my grandmother planned," she said quietly as they followed Maddy and Matt out of the house.

"I'm not, as I'm still going to have the pleasure of your company this evening," Joe told her. "Now, loosen up and pretend I'm fascinating, all right?"

"What?" Jessie asked, stopping dead on the front porch. "I don't think you understood me, Mr. O'Malley."

"Joe," he said, holding up his hand to correct her.

"You know who you are," Jessie said, gathering up her professionalism and trying to apply it to this truly insane situation. "I will not be a party to this ludicrous plan of yours and Allie's, and I told her so this morning. Now I'm telling you. Maddy is my sister and I love her. She's happy with Matt, so why don't you just fold up your mansion and steal away, or whatever."

"Yes, they are happy with each other, aren't

they?'' Joe agreed, looking at the happy couple as
they walked across the lawns, skirting the end of the
split rail fence. ''Just like brother and sister. Or, if
I'm not too far off base, brother and sister-*in-law*.''

''You're not only off base, Mr. O'Malley,'' Jessie
said, her cheeks burning. ''You're completely out of
the ballpark.''

''Am I, Jessie?'' he asked, motioning for her to
precede him down the three steps to the driveway.
''I don't think so. And neither do you. As a matter
of fact, I'm the answer to all your prayers, aren't
I?''

''I would never do anything to hurt my sister.
Never.''

''And I'm not asking you to, Jessie. Neither Almira nor I are asking you to do anything remotely
like that.''

''Then what are you asking me?''

Joe smiled, knowing he'd won at least this one
battle, even without Almira's help. ''I'm just asking
you to smile at me a time or two tonight, let me
smile back at you. Maybe lean our heads together,
whisper a time or two. Then you can look at your
sister, see if she's also smiling, or if she's doing a
slow burn, looking like she's ready to sink a steak
knife into my heart.''

''And if she is? Looking ready to kill you, that
is?''

''Ah, then you'll know she still loves me, just as
I still love her. That should ease your conscience
when I ask you to come over to my house tomorrow
to help me decide on curtain materials or whatever
excuse I can come up with at such short notice.''

Jessie bit her lip, watching as Maddy and Matt

walked along, not even holding hands. She'd seen movies of sailors walking the plank with more enthusiasm.

What was going on? Was Maddy having second thoughts? Was Matt?

Was she?

"Arranging furniture," she said at last, giving in to Joe's persuasive manner, to her own hopes. "That sounds more plausible."

Joe pulled her against his shoulder, giving her a hug. "That's my girl. I'm going to enjoy having you as a sister-in-law."

"You're unbelievably sure of yourself, aren't you...Joe?"

"Made me what I am today, Jessie," he told her, taking her hand in his as they approached the car. "I don't suppose you'd agree to hand-feeding me oysters out of the half-shell at dinner tonight? Or maybe that's just a little over the top."

Jessie giggled in spite of herself, and Maddy stiffened, frowned.

Joe opened the front passenger door for Jessie and smiled over the top of the car, looking into the slowly setting sun. Yup, it was going to be a real fun evening....

Chapter Seven

*I*f he smiles at her like that one more time, I'm going to lose my dinner, Maddy thought, pushing her fork so hard against her plate that the tines began to bend. *And what's Jessie doing, anyway? Giggling at every word Joe says? Jessie's giggling? Jessie never giggles. Never!*

But Jessie was giggling. She was smiling, laughing, having the time of her life. So was Matt.

In fact, everybody was so happy, so full of bright chatter that she could have cheerfully strangled each and every one of them. Her sister, her fiancé, her nemesis. The Three Joke-ateers.

How did a person make jokes about prime rates and megabytes? What was so blasted hilarious about a customer calling the help line to say that his cup holder broke on his computer? Oh, wait. Joe had explained that one to her. The guy was using the CD receptacle tray for his coffee cup. Ha. Ha, ha, ha. This was what passed for computer humor?

Well, okay. So it was a little funny. Just a little. She'd even smiled, in spite of herself. She understood computers; she'd used one at college, used one now to keep track of her recipes, used the World Wide Web to visit a very good home gardening site.

But computers were like automobiles. At least to Maddy they were. As long as the thing moved when she wanted, took her where she wanted to go, she saw no need to know more about computers or cars than where to slide the floppy disk, where to insert the gas. What went on under the hood, or beneath the bright aqua plastic computer monitor—well, she really couldn't care less.

And as for federal interest rates, stocks and bonds, tax free municipal bonds? Double ha. She'd have as much luck trying to understand how to split the atom. And about as much interest in the subject.

Which made her—what? Not at all a proper wife for a software king? Not at all a proper wife for a banker?

Maddy sighed, wishing she'd ordered dessert. Maybe two desserts. And Irish coffee. Not for the liquor. For the whipped cream. In fact, another couple of meals like this one, and they could just *roll* her to the table and let her graze.

Maddy looked at her sister from beneath her eyelashes. Jessie was positively *blooming*. Both men were paying attention to her, nodding their agreement with her every statement, going out of their way to listen, to comment, to tell her without words that she was scintillating company.

While ignoring Maddy. How rude.

Okay, so Matt had asked her if her prime rib was done to her liking.

That was it.

And it was all Joe's fault, damn him. He was the one who kept asking questions, setting off into new areas of conversation—all of which interested Maddy so little that after a while she didn't even bother trying to keep up or add her own opinion.

And he'd done it on purpose. She could tell. She could read the man like a book with only two pages. The Table of Contents, and the only chapter: *Joe O'Malley, why he thinks everybody should love him.*

Love him? She wanted to fricassee his liver. Pickle his kidneys. Slice his tongue, cold, for lunch.

And Matt was just as bad. Not that he was exactly *fawning* over Joe, but he certainly couldn't be nicer to the guy if he tried. All right, so Joe O'Malley was big news. Software genius and all of that. And probably with great big bags of money he might want to put into Matt's bank. So what?

Then there was her sister. Maddy's mind had to go back to Jessie, because Jessie was acting so strangely, so very much out of character, that she'd wondered if maybe someone had slipped a double shot of booze into her single vodka tonic. The giggling was one thing, but she was also touching her hair a lot, flipping it back behind her ears. Pressing her fingers against Joe's arm when she spoke to him; so very touchy-feely, which wasn't the usually controlled Jessie at all.

Maddy flagged down the waiter pushing the dessert cart around and selected a thin slice of sin described as Death By Chocolate Mud Pie. "And what a way to go," the waiter said, winking at her as he placed the plate in front of her, then spooned a large portion of freshly whipped cream beside the mud pie. "Enjoy."

"Maddy," Jessie said, her eyes wide as she looked at the plate. "Tell me you're not going to eat that."

Maddy felt her temper, on simmer all evening, getting ready to come to a full boil. *Ignore me all through dinner, then just when I'm doing something I shouldn't, you notice me? Thanks a heap, sis.* "No, Jessie, I'm not going to eat this. I only ordered it so I'd have someone to talk to. First that nice waiter, and now you. See how it works?"

Matt slid his arm behind Maddy's back, resting it on the top of the leather chair. "I'm sorry, Maddy. We've been ignoring you, haven't we?"

Maddy put her fork into the pie, twisted it around, mashing the chocolate even smoother. "It's all right. It isn't every evening us small-town folk have a chance to talk with the great J. P. O'Malley." She smiled at Joe across the table. "I guess I'm just not in the same league with Matt and Jessie, Joe. I'm much more interested in less exciting things, although I suppose talking about importing ladybugs to keep the insect population in my gardens down isn't really acceptable dinner table conversation."

You used to listen to me for hours and ask damn intelligent questions, Joe thought even as he smiled and apologized for excluding her from the conversation. "Personally," he added, "I think ladybugs are cute. Remember that old rhyme? 'Ladybug, ladybug, fly away home—'"

"'Your house is on fire, your children will burn,'" Jessie finished for him. "I don't know. The whole thing seems fairly depressing to me. But, then, most fairy tales are. I can remember staying up most of the night with bad dreams after my mother read me the story about the Three Pigs."

"Who did you feel sorry for, Jessie?" Joe asked, slipping *his* hand behind *her* chair. "The piggies, or the wolf?"

"The wolf ended up coming down the chimney of the brick house and falling straight into the cook pot, right?" Maddy said before slipping her tongue out to lick a small dollop of whipped cream from her upper lip. "Seems a fitting end for a big, bad wolf."

Joe grabbed the brass knob top of the chair back and squeezed, hard. She was deliberately driving him insane. "Remind me never to cross you, Maddy," he said, winking at Matt. "You might want to remember that, too, Matt."

"I'll be sure not to get too close to the stove," Matt said, and everyone laughed. Again. Everyone but Maddy.

Wasn't this all just *so* wonderful? Now, instead of laughing and talking and excluding her, they were laughing and talking *about* her. Gee, if she had any more fun tonight, she might just have to call Matt's sister and get a prescription for megadoses of Prozac.

"I hate to break up what has been a...wonderful evening," she said as Joe took a bite of lemon sherbet from the spoon Jessie offered him, "but Allie really wore me out today. I have a terrible headache."

"And a hive on the side of your neck," Joe supplied helpfully. "It's a good thing I reminded you to take a pass on wine, since it looks like you're going to need some antihistamines, poor thing. You get these hives often?''

Only when you leave or come back into my life, Maddy wanted to say, but didn't. ''Mrs. Ballantine thinks I'm reacting to the stiff netting material in the slips I need to wear beneath my gown,'' she said, her voice level, her green eyes shooting fire straight at Joe. ''Nothing but a temporary annoyance. Nothing, in fact, that won't go away forever directly after the wedding next week.''

Matt signaled to their waiter that he wanted the check, then looked from his fiancée to Joe O'Malley, wondering just what he was missing. Because he was missing something, that was for sure. Maddy was never impolite, and he'd certainly never seen her in a sulk before tonight. He'd tried, half a dozen times or more, to draw her into the conversation, but she had slipped back into silence each time, after only a monosyllabic response.

Maybe she did have a headache. Or maybe she didn't like Joe O'Malley. Which was ridiculous. He was a nice guy. Open, funny, friendly. And he seemed to enjoy Jessie's company a lot. That was good. Jessie needed to get out more, to stop being so damn devoted to her work in the family clothing manufacturing business. The work, he'd decided, that was her life, her only real interest.

Matt wished he could have gotten to know Jessie better, but even though he'd initially been very attracted to her, he knew that they also had very different goals in life. Jessie wanted a career; he wanted a home, a family. Jessie was married to her career. And he was about to marry her sister.

''Come on, Maddy,'' he said, standing up and

pulling out her chair after getting back his credit card from the waiter. "Let's get you and your headache home for a good night's sleep."

"We'll drop you off," Joe said, following them out of the restaurant, his right hand against Jessie's spine, guiding her along beside him. "Jessie and I are going to go back to my house for a while. She promised to help me arrange some furniture, didn't you, Jess?"

"Not *arrange,* Joe," Jessie said, her head sort of light, a pleasant buzzing in her ears. She'd never liked vodka, but tonight the drink had gone down quite easily, and to some effect. "I'll suggest and point. *You'll* be moving the furniture."

Everybody laughed. Ha. Ha, ha, ha.

Everybody but Maddy.

Joe wondered if he'd gone too far, pushed too hard. Maddy's little face had been white and pinched as he stood outside the car in front of the Chandler house and watched Matt walk her to the door.

Now, after taking Jessie home once they had actually arranged the living room furniture—Jessie having said something about not wanting to tell one more lie tonight—he found himself avoiding the white split rail fence and, instead, turning right, heading into the gardens behind the Chandler house.

He wasn't quite sure what he was doing. Maybe he just wanted to look up at the lights still burning on the third floor, moon around in the garden like some lovesick schoolboy hoping to catch a glimpse of his one true love.

Or maybe he wanted to find some small stones,

toss them up at the window, ask Maddy if she wanted to come out and play.

Or maybe he was just plain nuts.

He'd hurt Maddy tonight, and he'd known just what he was doing. That made him the louse her brother Ryan had called him. In spades.

It didn't matter how much he tried to tell himself he was doing all of this for Maddy's own good, that she'd never be happy married to Matthew Garvey.

Garvey was a good guy. A little stiff, slightly starchy, but a good guy. He did seem to genuinely care for Maddy.

But the guy wasn't hungry for her. He didn't look at her as if he might pick her up at any moment, toss her over his shoulder and take her somewhere to make love to her until they both were too exhausted to do more than curl up together and dream of each other.

Matthew Garvey didn't have that kind of passion in him. At least, he didn't seem to have it for Maddy. What he had for her, Joe had decided long before the salad course, was respect, admiration, a feeling of shared goals.

All that good stuff.

But without love? Without that grand passion? Without the heartbreaking, lifesaving passion, their lives would just be roles they played out, like *Ozzie and Harriet*, or those actors on *Father Knows Best*. Genuine liking, chaste kisses, twin beds, and vegetable soup for lunch.

How much better to be Lucy and Desi, he thought, keeping to his rather lame sitcom analogy. Lucy and Desi had *passion*. They fought, yes, but they loved. They really and truly *loved*.

If Joe and Maddy married—*when* they married—theirs would be a Lucy and Desi marriage. Hot, spicy. Never dull. Always with the passion...the passion.

If Matt and Maddy married?

Vegetable soup.

"Okay, you've convinced yourself, O'Malley," he said out loud. "Now convince her."

"Who's out there?"

Damn. Joe had been walking, and thinking. Not thinking about where he was walking. Certainly not too smart, either, speaking out loud as he had done. He lifted his head to realize that he had somehow come to be standing right outside the first-floor windows at the rear corner of the house, windows that allowed light to spill out onto the grounds, light that illuminated Maddy's body as she stood just outside a pair of opened French doors.

She was wearing soft blue cotton knit pajamas covered in a small riot of screen-printed, fluffy white Persian kittens. And she looked just as cuddly, with her hair falling loose around her shoulders, her red-tipped toenails peeking out from the too-long pajama trousers. Cat pajamas, and she looked sexy as hell. Go figure.

"Hi, babe." Joe stepped out of the shadows into one long splash of light. "Would you believe I was out hunting ladybugs?" he offered, hands in his pockets as he shrugged his shoulders and tried to look innocent.

Maddy released a pent-up breath, shifted her weight onto one bare foot and jammed a fist against her hip. "You."

Joe ducked his head as if avoiding an expected

slap, then walked closer. "You know, Mad, that's the third time you've greeted me that way. *You.* Yet each time it's been different. The first time, it was *you*—but sounded like *bastard.* The second time, it was *you*—but sounded more like *oh, no, not you.* Now, the third time, it sorta sounds like *oh, you. Figures.* I can't say I'm real flattered about any of those greetings."

"Gee, I could just cry for you," Maddy said, turning her back on him and quickly padding into the small drawing room. "Wait out there, let me get you a cookie. Then you can just go to—"

His hands were on her shoulders, stopping her voice, stopping her heart. He'd followed her inside. Of course he had. Of course she'd known he would. "Get out, Joe. Just get out, okay? Out of my house, out of my life."

"I just got back in it, Maddy."

"Yes, you did, didn't you?" she said, bending her knees to step out from beneath his hands, then turning to glare at him. "Aren't I the lucky one. And that performance tonight? I should have been handing out Oscars, to both you *and* my loving sister."

"Overacted, huh? I thought so," Joe said, taking another step forward, making a face that used to always produce a grin from Maddy, then a kiss. "Overacted, and overdone. I wanted to make you jealous, Maddy. I didn't plan to hurt you. But I did, didn't I?"

Maddy looked him straight in the eyes. "No, you didn't hurt me, Joe. You can't hurt me because I don't care about you. I don't care what you do, what you think, where you live, *how* you live. But Jessie is another matter. I never thought she could do something so mean to me."

"It was my idea, Mad, not Jessie's. And I think the double vodka tonic helped get her into the role. Please don't be angry with her. She's only trying to help a lovesick guy down on his luck."

"That being you, I suppose," Maddy said, walking over to one of the long tables covered in white linen and decorated with wedding gifts. With her back to him, she asked, "Do you really think Jessie believes I should be with you?"

"I don't know, Maddy," Joe answered, walking over to stand beside her, picking up one of a pair of silver candlesticks and testing its weight. "I suppose you'd have to ask her."

Maddy bit her bottom lip. "I thought—*think*—she's happy for me. She never said anything to make me think she didn't believe Matt and I were suited for…"

"Yes?" Joe urged when her words trailed off. "You were going to say *suited for each other,* weren't you? Not that you and Matt are wildly in love, can't live without each other, don't even want to live without each other. You know, Maddy, all that stuff we used to say to each other. Just suited for each other? Doesn't exactly make your heart go pitter-patter, does it? Suited for each other. I think I'll take what we had, personally."

Maddy took the candlestick from him, replaced it beside its mate. "That was different. That was lust. We fell in lust, Joe. And maybe in love, a little bit. But it couldn't last. Not with you making all the decisions, keeping those decisions from me. Lying to me, not trusting me."

"Second verse, same as the first," Joe grumbled, his hands drawing into impotent fists at his sides. "God, how I wish I could go back and do it over. Do it all over."

"Would you have done anything differently? Would you really?"

He considered her questions, honestly considered them. Then he shook his head. "No. No, I wouldn't have. You didn't trust in my conviction that Larry and I had a viable product, a future. That hurt, Mad, but I figured if I could just get us married, the rest of it would all work out."

"But you wouldn't take a penny from me. Wouldn't let me touch my trust fund, talk to Ryan about releasing some funds."

"I wouldn't ask Mother May I from your brother, no," Joe admitted, then figured he might as well say it all, every last damning word. "But I wanted to, Maddy. You don't know how much I wanted to take that money."

Maddy kept her head averted, pretending her knees weren't melting as she stood so close to Joe, as she smelled him, remembered the taste of him. "So why didn't you?"

His smile was wry, and rather sad. "You still don't get it, do you, babe? I wanted this to be me, on my own. Just the way I did it. Just the way I've always done everything."

"Just the way I've never done anything," Maddy added, spreading her arms, indicating this single opulent room in her opulent, well-cushioned, safe life. "We're two very different people, Joe, from two very different worlds. And even worse, you're the other type of person. The roller-coaster type."

That brought Joe's head up. "Say what? The roller-coaster type?"

She nodded, walked across the width of the Oriental carpet to stand in front of yet another long pedestal table burdened with dozens of wedding gifts. "I know it sounds rather simplified, Joe, but I've done a lot of thinking about us over the past eighteen months, and I've decided that there are two kinds of people in this world. The ones who ride the roller coaster, and the ones who don't."

He followed after her in a meandering way, walking around the perimeter of the room, looking at all the gifts, knowing he hadn't gotten her one yet, didn't even want to think about getting her one she'd share with Matt. "I like roller coasters, Maddy. Always have."

She smiled sadly. "Of course you do. You're the type that would. The type that thinks of nothing but the thrill of the ride. The type that figures bad things only happen to other people and the ride will be fun, and exhilarating, and nobody is going to get hurt. I'm the other type, the type that believes the roller coaster is just patiently sitting there, waiting for me to get on it so the damn thing can jump the track on the first steep hill."

"That's pretty black and white, Maddy," Joe told her, slowly making his way toward her, stopping a "safe" three feet away from her. "And pretty sad, too. Is that why you said yes to Matt? Because you're pretty sure he'd never run off the track? Is that why he asked you to marry him? I mean, I don't want to hurt you, Maddy, but there's not an awful lot of *spark* between the two of you. Anyone would think you've already been married for ten years."

Maddy lifted her chin, that adorable pointed chin. "Ha, a lot *you* know, Joseph O'Malley. Matt and I make mad, passionate love every night of the week."

"Just not tonight," Joe said, grinning. He didn't know why, but he was feeling better, more upbeat, by the minute. Considering the direction of their conversation, that made him either the world's greatest optimist or a man who obviously had no grasp on reality. "And not last night, either. Maybe not even tomorrow night. Maybe—could it be— *never?*"

"Oh, shut up," Maddy ordered, wishing she hadn't stooped so low as to involve Matt in some sort of contest with her former lover. Her only lover...but Joe wasn't ever going to know *that* one.

"Agreed," Joe said. "We'll change the subject, and never bring it up again. I mean, after all, I'm off the roller coaster now, just another safe, solvent corporate genius, and you're going to marry Matthew Garvey, and never even *look* at the roller coaster, wonder if you'd missed anything by not taking a chance, taking that ride. So, what will we talk about? Ah, here's a conversation piece if I ever saw one."

Maddy looked on as Joe picked up the Thing, examining it as he carefully turned it in his hands.

"Well, babe," he said at last, "you might not have ridden the roller coaster lately, but you sure did go to the fair. You got this for fooling the weight-guessing guy, right? Or maybe Matt rang the bell three times on the test your strength game? Scratch that. You'd get this big beauty for losing, not for winning."

Maddy snatched the vase from his hands. "This is a genuine *Nove*, given to me by my Great-Aunt Harriet. It's worth thousands."

"Right. Sure." Joe's blue eyes twinkled. "Thousands of what, Maddy? So, what did you ever do to Great-Aunt Harriet to tick her off this bad?"

Maddy bit her lip, trying not to laugh. She'd known when she'd first looked at the Thing that Joe would have something funny to say about it. "I don't know," she admitted at last. "I always thought I was her favorite. Just goes to show you that we don't know everything, doesn't it?"

Joe picked up the vase once more. "I guess you could keep popcorn in it, something like that."

"Popcorn? I guess that is one option. I was going to give it to Allie, but she threatened to cut me out of her will."

"I like your grandmother. Smart lady," Joe said, then belatedly realized that their too-short moments of being at ease with each other, of even bantering back and forth with each other, had just ended. They'd ended the moment Almira Chandler's name had been introduced in the conversation.

"She shouldn't have contacted you, Joe. And you shouldn't have listened to her, shouldn't have come. I'm going to marry Matt. I've made up my mind."

"Ozzie and Harriet do Allentown. Yawn," Joe mumbled beneath his breath, shaking his head.

"What? What did you say?"

"Never mind, Maddy, I was just talking to myself. So," he added, spreading his hands as if to try to gather up the correct words with which to say good-night. Say goodbye. "I guess I ought to get going. My computer stuff is coming tomorrow, and I'm going to spend most of the day setting it up.''

''Your toys,'' Maddy said, her smile slow and somewhat sad. ''I remember. Did you ever get that desk you dreamed about? The one that you said would be a complete circle, with a lift-up bar so you could go in and out, sit surrounded by your toys, safe in computer heaven?''

He nodded. ''I had one specially built last year. I'm surprised you remember that dream, among so many I bent your ears with while we were together.''

''I remember all your dreams, Joe,'' Maddy said, walking toward the door, so that he had no choice but to follow after her. ''And now I have some of my own.''

He took her right hand in his, ran his thumb over her fingertips—her cold as ice fingertips, even though the night was warm. ''Dreams I'm not in, right?''

''You were,'' she said, sighing. ''Once upon a time.''

''Another sad fairy tale.'' He squeezed her fingers, sighed, then let her go. ''I haven't thrown in the towel yet, Maddy. We still could have our happily ever after. If you'll just give me a chance. Don't tell me my stupid pride has left it too late.''

''Your pride, my pride. What does it matter, Joe? I thought I loved you, once. Now I'm not so sure. I'm not sure what love is at all, or if it even exists. I just know that I've planned my life, gotten my priorities straight maybe for the first time in that life. I'm content, Joe. Or at least I was, until you came barging back in my life, courtesy of Allie. Now I want you to go away again, leave me to do what I've chosen as the best thing for me.''

"And the best thing for Matt? Does he know you don't love him?"

"I do so—" Maddy pressed her lips together, knowing she couldn't say she loved Matt, not when she'd just admitted that she didn't even know what love was. But she did know the pain of loss, and she never wanted to put herself in a position to feel that sort of pain again. "Go home, Joe. It's late."

He looked down at her, saw the tears pooling in her eyes, saw the hurt he'd put there eighteen months ago and again tonight. He wanted to kiss her, wanted to pull her into his arms and hold her, love her, promise he'd never make her cry again.

But he didn't.

He simply lifted a hand to her cheek, traced his thumb along her cheekbone, down to the tip of her kissable chin, turned and walked out into the night.

Chapter Eight

"In layman's terms, Maddy, they're called signature hives. Doesn't make them itch any less, but they're not dangerous, I promise."

Maddy nodded as she pulled down her knit top after showing her rather red and bumpy back to Dr. Linda Garvey, Matt's sister. The two were in one of Linda's examination rooms, after Maddy had phoned early that morning, begging help. "So what you're saying is I'm not terminal," she said, trying her best to smile. Which wasn't easy. Not with this darn fat lip. "I suppose that's a relief."

"You *suppose* it's a relief?" Linda repeated. "Well, I guess that answers my next question, which was how well the antihistamines are working on those hives. Itch like hell, don't they?"

Maddy hopped down from the examining table, not liking the feeling she had when sitting there, not liking to feel at all like a patient. Which was all Joe's fault. If he hadn't gone out to dinner with them...if he hadn't all but drooled on Jessie...if he hadn't shown up later, to talk, to argue...to make her remember. "Around three o'clock this morning I began giving serious thought to rubbing myself down with sandpaper."

"Ouch!" Linda looked up from the prescription she was writing. "Pretty drastic treatment, Maddy. I think I can do at least a little better than that." She ripped off two prescriptions, handed them to her. "Here, try these. Sort of my two-shot treatment, pills and cream. If you're not a whole lot better in twenty-four hours, though, please feel free to give me another call. At home if it's after hours—you know the number. And, Maddy?"

"Hmm?" Maddy said, trying to read Linda's chicken scratches. Must be one of the prerequisites for graduation for doctors: Illegible Writing 101. When Linda didn't go on, she looked up at her, saw her motion for her to take a seat in the chair beside the examining table.

Linda pulled a round, wheeled stool out for herself, and sat down facing Maddy from across the small room. "Okay, so what's going on?"

Maddy averted her eyes from Linda's, whose own eyes looked so much like Matt's. "What's going on? Gee, I don't know, Linda. I'm getting married next week. We've got all the last minute running around, the meetings with florists and caterers and people I didn't even know existed, let alone knew were needed to pull off a proper garden wedding. Did you know that there are people who just rent out tents for a living? And, if you knew that—and I think I did, too—did you know how many different *kinds* of tents there are? Then there's seating plans, and photographers, thank-you notes I'm trying to keep up to date on, and…well, isn't that enough?''

"It's a lot, I will say that. Having long ago happily and quite eternally married myself to my career as a pill pusher, however, I never really thought about any of that before you mentioned it. But what else, Maddy? Because Matt told me all these plans are pretty well finalized, thanks to your mind-boggling efficiency, and have been for months. So— what else is going on? What's bothering you?''

Maddy scratched at her left forearm. She'd tell Linda almost anything. But she had never told her the truth, not eighteen months ago, and most definitely not now. "What's bothering me is these *hives!* I can't sleep, all I do is scratch, and no matter what I take, they get worse. If I lie down, they seem to subside for a while, but when I stand up again, they come back again. I actually stood in front of the bathroom mirror this morning and *watched* several dozen small ones pop out on my face. It's enough to drive anyone a little wacko.''

"Or being driven a little wacko is enough to give someone hives,'' Linda said carefully, incisively turning Maddy's own words back on her. "Oh, and don't think I swallowed that allergic to your tulle slips story, because I haven't. Those would be contact hives, and you don't wear slips on the end of your nose, you know. Besides, these are signature hives, and that's enough to set off some warning bells in my head.''

Maddy frowned. "I don't get it. What's so different about my hives? I thought you said they weren't dangerous.''

"They're not. The sort of hives you have, Maddy,

are a symptom. A symptom of stress. I had a gal in
here last week, covered in them. She thought she
was allergic to packing material she was using, but
that wasn't it. After talking to her for a while, learning that she'd bought a new house just to have the
sale on her present one fall through and that she was
looking at paying two mortgages for a while...well,
that finally explained the hives. Especially when I
traced the mark of a dollar sign on her thigh, just to
watch a hive come up in exactly that shape. Signature hives, Maddy. Understand now?''

"Oh. Yes, I guess I get it," Maddy said, sighing...then quickly lifted her hand from her thigh,
where she had begun idly tracing a fingernail over
her skin. "Damn. I shouldn't have done that."

Linda stood, walked over to look down at
Maddy's thigh below her plaid Bermuda shorts. The
hive had already begun, all three hives, as a matter
of fact. The letters were still faint, but readable.
"Joe? Who's Joe?"

"Joe?" Maddy said, quickly standing up, heading
for the door. "That wasn't Joe, Linda. That was...
that was toe. Yes, toe. I'm leaving here to get a
pedicure, and it was the first word that seemed to
come into my mind."

Linda, who had Matt's same caring blue eyes, but
had somehow missed out on his easier-going nature,
pointed a finger toward the chair and ordered: "Sit!
Speak!"

Maddy, shoulders slumping, retraced her steps to
the chair and sat down as ordered. "Are you going
to lock the door, not let me out until I talk? Yeah,
I guess you are. Professional confidence here,

Linda? I mean, like you can't repeat anything I say to you, patient to doctor. Right?''

''That's what they told me when they let me write Doctor in front of my name,'' Linda said, pushing a stray lock of hair behind her ear, tucking it close to the plain, no-nonsense bun she wore at her nape. ''Now, one more time, and try to go for the gusto, Maddy, and tell me all of it. Who's Joe?''

Maddy's face crumpled. It just…crumpled. Tears sprang into her eyes, not to be denied. ''Oh, Linda…I'm a mess!'' she exclaimed, reaching into the pocket of her shorts for the wad of tissues she'd shoved in there earlier, after the crying bout she'd had at home.

She swiped at her tears, then spread her hands, shook her head. ''Look at me. Just *look* at me! I haven't slept in two days, Linda, I'm eating myself right out of my wedding gown, and I *itch* all over. I've got bumps on my face, bumps on the soles of my feet, bumps on my butt, for crying out loud. I'm falling apart.''

Linda let her cry. Just sat and let her cry. Then, when Maddy seemed to be calming down, she retrieved some tissues from a cabinet, planning on handing some to her. Giving this idea a second thought, she simply passed over the entire box to her weepy friend. ''Okay, that was good, for a start. Now tell me something I don't know. Tell me about Joe.''

''I…I *can't!*'' Maddy said, hiccuping. ''I mean, you're Matt's *sister,* and I…''

Now Linda sat down herself, looking up at Maddy from the short stool. ''Hooboy,'' she said quietly.

"I have to admit I wasn't expecting that one. Came at me straight out of right field. Another man."

"No!" Maddy protested hotly. "There is *not* another man. Oh, all right, so there *was*...once...but there's not *now*...except that he's back, living right next door, so he *is* here...and I don't want him here because he's just confusing *everything*, telling me I should marry him instead of...well, you know... and...and living right next door, like I said... and...and...and giving me *hives*...and...and...and Allie is...Allie said...Allie—oh, you *know* Allie, Linda." She looked at her friend and doctor. "Oh, God, Linda, what am I going to do?"

As she did her best to decipher Maddy's ramblings, Linda's first, most immediate reaction, was to think of her brother, how he could end up very hurt, very shortly. But that thought didn't last long. It couldn't. Maddy was her patient, and she had to look at this entire situation in that confidential patient-doctor context.

Besides, Maddy was one of those people you just couldn't get mad at; it would be like getting mad at a flower for blooming. She was just Maddy. Simple, straightforward, sweet and cuddly Maddy. One of the world's good creatures; honest, kind, loyal. She also was one of those people things happened *to;* she never went out of her way to do anything to anybody else. She'd never hurt anyone on purpose. She'd rather cut off her own nose than hurt anyone else.

Or break out in hives from the top of her head to the soles of her feet...

"Maddy, may I tell you something you've probably figured out for yourself?" she asked.

"No, you're wrong," Maddy protested, sure of what Linda would say. "I started breaking out in hives before Joe showed up, Linda. At least a full hour before Allie dragged me to the window to see him moving into the Harris house. I had hives *before* he showed up."

"A full hour before he showed up, huh? That would have been while you were trying on your wedding gown, right? What else was going on, besides trying on the gown?"

Maddy tried to suck on her swollen upper lip. "Damn," she said at last, reaching for another tissue. "I had been thinking about what I'd worn the last time, and how I left Joe standing outside the Vegas wedding chapel eighteen months ago." She started slightly, looked at Linda. "Matt doesn't know about that. *Nobody* knows about that, except Jessie and Allie and Ryan."

Linda gave a few second's nostalgic thought to her notion, during high school, of becoming an astronaut. She should have done it. If she had, she wouldn't be sitting here, listening to her brother's fiancée say she had left another man at the altar eighteen months ago, and was probably about to leave her brother in the same ignominious position in another week. That was, unless she wanted to go through the rest of her life gulping down antihistamines.

"You can't do this, Maddy," she told her, writing out a new prescription and exchanging it for one of the two she'd previously handed over to her. "Never mind the anti-itch cream for now, okay? I'm giving you a strong antihistamine, and a small prescription for a nerve pill. Because, Maddy, my dear, it's either talk about all of this with Matt, or spend the rest of your life scratching your skin off, straight down to the bone.''

"Once we're married…'' Maddy began, then stopped, shook her head. "They're not going to go away? I'm going to spend the rest of my life with a fat lip?''

"Think of it this way, Maddy,'' Linda said, trying for a little humor. "You'll never have to worry about being without pen and paper when you want to make a note of something.'' When Maddy didn't laugh, but just reached for another tissue, Linda put her arm around her shoulders, gave her a squeeze. "Ah, honey, don't cry. But do tell the truth. It's the secret that's hurting you. The secret and, just maybe, a little indecision on your part. Until you examine what's going on, *and* get this all off your chest, well, I'm pretty sure you're going to have those hives. Modern medicine can do a lot, but it still hasn't been able to cure a guilty conscience.''

"Larry? Say something nice about me. Quick. Remind me that I'm kind to animals. That I give generously to charity. That I don't usually go around making women cry.''

Larry's voice—Loony Larry the bookkeeping genius's voice—traveled to Joe through the phone connection from Philadelphia. "Oh, brother. What did you do now?''

Joe shifted the portable phone to his other ear as he sat down on the chaise beside the pool. "Oh, I don't know, Lar. I showed up in Maddy's life without warning, bought the house next door to her.''

"Yeah, I know. Stupid move, but typically you. What else?"

"That isn't enough? Oh, okay, I'll give you all of it. Or did I already tell you she's getting married next week? Gee, guess not.''

It was always a good thing to put about two feet of air space between ear and phone when giving Larry this kind of news. Money kind of news. *"She what?"* Larry bellowed as Joe held the phone in front of him, saving his left ear to hear again another day. "Are you telling me you paid that *fortune* for a house next door to a woman who left you at the altar, damn near ruined your life—and she's getting *married* next week? Is that what you're telling me, Joe?"

There were a few moments of silence, just as predictable as Larry's vocal explosion, before he went on, more quietly, "Why'd you do that, Joe?"

"Because I'm an optimistic idiot?" Joe offered, sliding on his mirrored sunglasses as the glare of sun from the pool struck him straight in the eyes. "Because I thought she'd take one look at me and fall into my arms? Because I'll do anything, even something as stupid and asinine as buying a house, in order to get her attention? And she hates me, Lar. She's breaking out in hives, she hates me so much. Can you believe it? I'm in love with a woman and she breaks out in hives every time she lays eyes on me. I could actually watch them popping up on her chest last night when we were talking. She was wearing these damn pussycat pajamas that were too long for her, and her eyes were so wide and hurt, and I've been up all night, calling myself every rotten name in the book. So say something nice about me, okay?''

"I'm coming up there," Larry said shortly. "I'm coming up there, I'm going to find you a nice, safe padded room for the next couple of weeks. You'll be fine, Joe. I promise."

"You never liked her, did you?"

There was another silence. "I liked her, Joe," Larry said at last. "I liked her a lot. What's not to like? She's cute, she's sweet, and until she ditched you, I thought she might just have been the best thing that ever happened to you. Remember, Joe, I'd been trying to get you to go into business for two years, and you wouldn't take the chance until you decided that you wanted to have at least as much money in your jeans as your wife did. Without Maddy, God only knows if we'd be where we are now, leading the current wave of software wunderkinds. So, yeah, I like her. I just don't like what she did to you when she left. I mean, you weren't exactly easy to live with for a while there, and you know how I feel about working eighteen-hour days.''

"Time and a half for overtime," Joe said, smiling slightly. "Okay if it's you and me, but it really put a twist in your briefs when I started pushing everyone else that hard." Then the smile faded. "Lar, what am I going to do? Losing Maddy once nearly killed me. I can't lose her again."

"You haven't got her *to* lose her, buddy, not if she's about to marry someone else. And, if she loves him, you'd be the last person to interfere with her happiness. Right?"

"If she loves him," Joe agreed, looking over the trees dividing the two properties, looking straight at the third-floor windows of Maddy's apartment. She wasn't there, because he'd seen her drive off earlier, but just being in the backyard, able to see her windows, somehow made him feel better. Man, he really was losing it! "But I don't think she does, Lar, that's the thing. I mean, okay, she loves him. But she's not *in love* with him."

"Ah, the voice of sweet reason enters the conversation. Or would that be hopeful imagination?"

Sometimes Joe was happy that Larry was fourteen years his senior and, at forty-two, a saner, more levelheaded kind of guy—even if Maddy did privately call him Loony Larry. He'd kept Joe anchored through his most elaborate flights of fancy when developing their new software, even as he'd believed in Joe's ideas, encouraged him to dream. There was a *balance* about Larry Barry that just seemed to make it all work.

But there were times, like now, when Larry seemed to take on the role of Joe's long-absent father, using that simple seniority to make him feel ten years old. And selfish. And sometimes even dumb.

"I don't want her to make a mistake, Larry," Joe said now, hoping his voice sounded reasonable, not mean-spirited. "A mistake that would ruin three lives."

"Lives, hives," Larry shot back across the wires. "Gee, they even rhyme. Like I said, I'm coming up there. Now, stop with the wishful thinking, and give me directions."

"I didn't call you so you'd come running up here to hold my hand, Larry. I can take care of myself."

"Then why did you call me, kid?"

Joe was silent for a few moments. He knew why he'd called Larry, the guy he trusted, the guy with the level head and a bean counter mentality mixed with a liberal dab of compassion and a mountain of cherished friendship. He wasn't Joe's father, but he had been part father-figure, right from the beginning. Joe couldn't deny that, didn't want to deny that. And, if anyone could keep his head on straight as his heart broke, Joe knew that man to be Larry Barry.

"You take the Northeast Extension of the Turnpike, and then..."

It was gone noon when Jessie and Ryan pulled up chairs at the long conference table and spread out hamburgers and French fries delivered from a local diner. They'd been at work since eight, gone through at least a gallon of coffee each and planned to work through the noon hour, straight on until six o'clock. Or later.

It wasn't due to the end of their fiscal year, or because of any emergency. It was just because that was how they'd always done it. Everything for the company, to the exclusion of most everything else, including their private lives. But it was a family company and they were the family.

Jessie picked up a nearly half-inch stack of pink memo slips and began paging through them as she chewed on a French fry. "You know, Ryan, you really do have to start returning your calls. Melissa, Joanne, Beth, Missy—wait, is that still Melissa?

Nope, different phone number—Althea. Ooh, ooh, ooh, *Althea*. I thought she told you to drop dead because you broke so many dates in order to work late?''

Ryan shook salt onto his hamburger. "She did. Last month. But they all want to know who I'm escorting to Maddy's wedding. I've had Jan taking messages for the past three days, while offering the information that I'm going stag. Not that anyone seems to be taking the hint. So, Jessie, about the Fuller contract—''

"You idiot! You don't *tell* women you're going stag to anything," Jessie explained, tossing the phone messages into the trash. "That's like a red flag to a bull, or waving a candy bar under a kid's nose, or—''

"I think I get your point," Ryan interrupted, sitting back in his chair, running a hand through his hair. "I'll tell Jan."

"Do that," Jessie said, nodding. "Now, tell me why you're going stag? I mean," she ended with a gesture toward the trash can, "it's not like you couldn't get a date."

"I don't know, Jessie," he answered honestly. "I guess I'm just not in the mood to be fending off single ladies who want nothing more than to catch the next tossed bouquet."

"You're working too hard, brother," Jessie said, laughing. "I mean, you're *supposed* to be willing to catch all those lucky females for yourself, as they'll be in very *romantic* moods. Weddings are a single person's best friend, when it comes to looking forward to a night of romance."

Ryan picked up a spreadsheet, pretended to study

it. "Oh, yeah? I had no idea you were such an expert on these things. And who are *you* bringing, Jessie? Last I heard, you were going stag, too, claiming you'd be too busy with your maid of honor duties."

"We weren't talking about me," Jessie said shortly, picking up a spreadsheet from the pile beside her. Another Chandler trait—when in doubt, or when unable to think of a good enough lie to turn away disturbing thoughts, questions, Chandlers went to work. "But we probably should talk about Allie. She says J. P. O'Malley is her date for the rehearsal dinner."

"She wouldn't dare," Ryan said, wincing. "Scratch that, yes, she would. Damn it, why can't she just back off, leave well enough alone, just this one time? Anyone would think she didn't like Matt, which is ridiculous, because she adores him. And she's *supposed* to like Maddy a little, too, not that you could tell that from the way she's running around, screwing up that poor kid's life. I have to tell you, Jessie, I haven't felt so sorry for anyone in my life. The kid's a mass of nerves."

"Allie thinks she's doing it for the best," Jessie said, barely able to believe she was defending her grandmother's actions. But then, she knew Almira wasn't just trying to help Maddy see the error of her ways. She was also meddling in Matt's life, in hers. And Jessie, evil and rotten as she knew it was, had been secretly rooting like hell for her grandmother ever since she figured out what the woman, and her accomplice, Mrs. Ballantine, were up to.

"Allie thinks she does everything for the best. Like setting me up for that blind date last month. What a miserable evening that was, for the both of us. Although, come to think of it, since O'Malley showed up two days ago, she's been remarkably well-behaved. Now, if we only knew if that was a good thing or a bad thing.''

Jessie smiled weakly. "Or, thirdly, if we really want to know anything *at all*.''

Chapter Nine

Maddy finally drove home around three. She'd gone straight to the pharmacy to get her prescriptions filled, driven around aimlessly for about an hour because she couldn't think of anything better to do, then downed both pills with a bottle of spring water and a vegetarian, low-fat salad she'd picked at as she sat in a local restaurant, thinking over her life.

Was she supposed to take both pills at the same time? Linda had given her a bunch of instructions, and warnings, before Maddy had left the office, but she really hadn't been listening to her doctor with more than half an ear, even as she'd promised that she was hanging on every word.

Oh well, too late now, she thought, once again thinking about her life as she stabbed a large piece of romaine lettuce.

She had come to a few conclusions.

One, she was a mess. That was a given, considering her hives, considering the way she'd turned into a soggy, weeping mess in Linda's office.

Two, she was going to continue to be a mess until she made up her mind, told the truth, took a stand and regained some semblance of control over her own life.

And three, hey, these pills were kinda neat.

They were so neat, in fact, that Maddy kept the radio off and her eyes-wide open on the thankfully short drive home, talking to herself the whole time, because she was feeling way too mellow to pay attention to traffic otherwise.

But, hey, her hives were gone. The itch was gone. And there was this lovely little *glow* around everything in her pretty screwed up world.

Nice. Very nice. Artificial. Temporary. But very, very nice. Once she'd parked the car with even more than her usual care, she slipped into the house, and finally let her defenses down, at last allowing the medications to have their lovely way with her.

"Hi, Allie, you sweet thing," Maddy said as she all but waltzed into the main drawing room, her arms sort of floating somewhere at her sides, her grin wide, and happy for no reason at all. "How ya doin', Mrs. Ballantine? Shouldn't you two be in the kitchen, mixing up another witches' brew? I mean, you found Joe, brought him here to ruin my life. Maybe now you could conjure up Elvis, or pull a rabbit out of your ear. Pull a rabbit out of Elvis's ear?"

"Madeline Chandler," Almira said, pulling her granddaughter over to the nearest couch and pushing her down into it. "Don't tell me you've been *drinking*."

"Nope," Maddy said, hoping her grin was rather Cheshire-like, mysterious. "*Thinking*, yes, but not drinking. And you know what I've been thinking? Do you want to know? Huh? Huh, huh, huh? Okay! I've been thinking that superficial isn't so bad. So there."

"Coffee, right. Strong, black and lots of it," Mrs. Ballantine said as Almira looked to her. She walked toward the hallway. "I'm already on it."

"You know what I'm saying?" Maddy went on, oblivious to her grandmother's concern. "Superficial. Surface. No pain, no pain. That's how to be. No worrying, none of that guilt stuff, no crying...no decisions. Just, whee, isn't the sky a pretty blue, aren't those flowers just as red as red can be?"

She sighed, smiled, sagged against the couch cushions. "Nobody gets hurt, or if they do, I just don't notice. Especially about me. No pain, no pain. And Joe O'Malley can be as gorgeous and sexy and wonderful as he wants to be. I just don't care, so there."

She looked up at her grandmother. "Are there any cookies left in the kitchen? I'm hungry for something sweet. Rabbits eat lettuce. Rabbits, and maybe Elvis. But I want sugar. I'm cute pudgy. Everybody says so." She frowned slightly. "I don't know that Elvis was, though...." She brightened again. "But think of all the new employment opportunities for overweight men with sideburns."

"Maybe she's having some sort of spell. Maybe I pushed too hard. I'm calling Linda Garvey, asking her to come over here," Almira said to herself, walking past the heavy-lidded Maddy as she headed for the nearest phone.

Ten minutes later, Maddy was sitting up with no small amount of help from Mrs. Ballantine while Almira spoon-fed her strong, black coffee.

"So, yes, it turns out Dr. Garvey already saw Maddy in her office this morning," Almira explained calmly, for the second time. "For the hives, you understand. Linda says lack of sleep probably combined with the medicines to put the poor thing over the edge, although she wasn't supposed to take the other medication until she got home."

"Do you think she listened?" Mrs. Ballantine asked, her voice incongruously soft and caring. Not at all the drill sergeant.

"We both rather think she didn't listen to Linda too well," Almira told Mrs. Ballantine as Maddy grinned, and slurped coffee, and then began singing snatches of a song that had something to do with the moon and blue and June. "And it would seem Maddy's system doesn't handle some medications as well as others. So, first a little coffee, then bed, then no more doses of anything but the antihistamine. Linda said a few hours of uninterrupted sleep is the best cure for everything that ails Maddy right now, not that I could get the woman to tell me just what is ailing Maddy, except for the hives."

"Bed," Maddy said on a sigh, leaning her head against Mrs. Ballantine's arm. "'Perchance to dream…'"

Mrs. Ballantine, in full Mother Lion mode, snorted disdainfully. "You really had to ask? *You're* what's bothering Miss Maddy, Mrs. Chandler. You and your meddling and scheming. That's as plain as the nose on my face. I'm embarrassed to be a part of it."

Almira winced. "Your nose, huh? And God knows that's plain enough. Yes, well, she'll be fine with a few hours sleep. There's been no real harm done."

"What had she been taking? Only antihistamines?" Mrs. Ballantine asked as she carefully laid Maddy down on the couch, removed her shoes, covered her with a cashmere throw. Maddy began to snore. "Did Dr. Garvey say?"

Almira, who knew darn full well Linda must have prescribed some sort of nerve pill for her youngest, most volatile grandchild, but who still needed the protective Mrs. Ballantine as her ally in the Marriage Wars, said only, "I didn't ask, and she didn't say. Probably some sort of double-dose for the hives and the itching. There, she's asleep. We'll let her rest for a while before we put stage two of our plan into effect."

Mrs. Ballantine ruffled up like a huge black crow about to let loose with a great big squawk. "I can't condone this, Mrs. Chandler. I've gone this far, but to go further? Look at her," she commanded, flinging out one wing...er, *arm*...to indicate the softly snoring Maddy. "She's down and out, miserable. Confused. Falling apart."

Almira looked at her granddaughter. "Yes, you're right, Mrs. Ballantine. She's all of that. And I can't think of a better time to give her another gentle push."

"Where to? Off a cliff?"

"No, you fainthearted excuse for a conspirator. Not off a cliff. Straight into Joe O'Malley's arms, where we both know she belongs. She does, too, although she won't admit it."

"You're that sure?"

"I'm that sure," Almira said, handing Mrs. Ballantine the coffee cup. She walked out of the room, head held high, before the housekeeper could see the worried frown she couldn't hide. She wanted this over, now. Sooner than now. Before she began to doubt what she was doing.

Maddy woke as the small brass mantel clock chimed the hour of four. She lay on her back for a few minutes, wondering how on earth she'd ended up on the sofa with a soft cashmere throw over her. The logical conclusion was that she'd come home, laid down and taken a nap. Which was very odd, because she never took naps.

The pills, she realized a few moments later, wincing at her own stupidity. Well, that certainly answered the question of whether or not she'd been supposed to take both of them at the same time, didn't it?

Still, she felt so rested, so much more calm, even a little bit in control of herself. After the events of the past two days, that was really saying something.

"Ah, you're awake," Almira said from somewhere in the room, and Maddy looked across the wide expanse to see her grandmother walking toward her. "I've been sitting here, trying to understand how any granddaughter of mine could possibly snore. Must have gotten it from your mother's side, that's all I can say."

Maddy pushed a lock of hair out of her face. "I do *not* snore," she countered in sudden embarrassment. "Do I?"

"Only when drugged, I'd imagine," Almira told

her, making scooting motions with her right hand, so that Maddy put her feet on the floor, leaving room on the sofa for her grandmother to sit down beside her. "Now, are we going to talk about this, or are we going to pretend it never happened? I'm open to either one, although I will tell you, just to be fair, that I've already spoken to Linda Garvey."

"You *did?* She did? She talked to you? But she promised she wouldn't—" Maddy was fully awake now, completely alert. "Oh, wait a minute. Wait just one darn minute. You're on a fishing expedition, aren't you, Allie? Linda didn't tell you anything."

"Busted," Almira said, grinning as she leaned over to kiss Maddy's cheek. "But I am a pretty good guesser. Don't take any more of those pills, darling, because you don't really need them. Not for what ails you right now anyway. They only hide problems, they don't solve them. Only you can solve them. You're lucky that way. You *do* know what your problems are, don't you?"

Maddy got to her feet, stretched as she smiled down at Almira. "You mean after *you,* Allie?" she asked. "I mean, world peace would be easier to achieve than trying to keep you from meddling in my life."

"Thank you, darling," Almira said as she, too, rose, "but don't give me too much credit. You're doing a pretty good job of complicating your life yourself, aren't you?"

Maddy wasn't about to admit anything of the kind, true as it was. Instead she spread her arms wide, then dropped them firmly to her sides once more, saying, "Well, that was fun. My turn again, I believe. New subject, please."

"Same subject, new problem," Almira said, retrieving her purse and car keys from a nearby table. "I promised Joe I'd wait for the television cable person to come sometime between four and six today. And I would have, except that Jessie phoned and said I have to come down to the plant and sign a few things. Quarterly bonus checks for our best employees, I believe, so I imagine I shouldn't put it off until tomorrow."

She reached into the pocket of her rose pink linen suit, extracted a single key, the one Maddy recognized as being their emergency key to the Harris house. "Joe's in Philadelphia, doing big shot computer genius things, I suppose, and won't be home until late tonight, so you're safe."

Maddy took the key, looked at it as if it might turn into a finger-eating lizard or something. "Let me get this straight. *You* volunteered to house-sit while waiting for the cable guy? *You?* Uh-huh," she said, holding out the key. "Not buying that one, Allie, not this time. You wouldn't even baby-sit us kids, let alone a house."

Almira put on her "stern" face, one she didn't wear often. "I don't have time to stand here and listen to some litany of my shortcomings before your parents died, or whatever it is you're trying to say, or attempting to blame on me. Go over there and wait, or stay here. I really couldn't care less."

She strode out of the room, not looking back, leaving Maddy still holding the key.

"Well," Maddy said to no one in particular, "if I didn't know the woman so well, I'd think I just insulted her."

"You said something, Miss Maddy?" Mrs. Ballantine asked, coming into the room, carrying a large feather duster with her, trailing it over pieces of furniture as she went. "How are you feeling?"

"Oh, I'm fine, thank you. Really much better," Maddy said, and realized that she was right. She did feel better. Sharper. Sharp enough to see a trick when it was presented to her. "I'm supposed to go next door to wait for the cable guy to hook up Mr. O'Malley's television cable, but I don't think I want to. But you think I should go, don't you?"

"Me?" Mrs. Ballantine asked, shaking her head. "Why would I care about something like that, Miss Maddy? But, if you don't have time, I'll be happy to do it for you. I'd like to see what Mr. O'Malley has done with the place so far. Ask me, he should paint all those dark walls white, and start from there."

"You...you'd go in my place?"

"It *is* cold-cuts night, remember? I have nothing much to do here anyway, as we won't be serving in the dining room."

Was Mrs. Ballantine telling the truth? About the cold-cuts, sure. But what about being willing to take Maddy's place? Was she being nice, or was she being devious? Had Allie put the woman up to this whole charade? Was it a charade?

Did she care?

"Never mind, Mrs. Ballantine," Maddy said, already heading out of the room. "I'll take care of it."

"Very good, Miss Maddy," Mrs. Ballantine called after her, then weakly subsided into a chair. This intrigue and reverse-psychology stuff wasn't easy....

* * *

If she'd been sent over to Joe's to spy on him, report back what he'd done to the Harris house, Maddy would have precious little to say. There was furniture in a few of the downstairs rooms, but other than in the living room, the furniture was just sort of piled up here and there, awaiting arranging.

Jessie had helped in the living room. She'd done a good job. A really good job. Maddy stood with her chin in her hand, admiring the scene for long moments through the eyes of a woman who'd scored an *A* in her Interior Design class, then deliberately moved the blue chair closer to the window. "Better," she said, knowing she was being petty.

She should sit down. Maybe on the blue chair. Sit down, wait…mind her own business.

That thought stayed with her as she walked through to the kitchen, opened the refrigerator and pulled out a can of sarsaparilla soda, popped the top and took a long drink.

Her stomach growled an indignant protest, reminding Maddy that all she'd had to eat today had been a salad, telling her that sarsaparilla soda was okay for starters, but it wasn't meat and potatoes.

So she made herself a peanut butter and jelly sandwich. Munched on it as she walked back through the house, pretending she wasn't really looking into every room, imagining every room complete, yes, down to painting over all the dark wallpaper the Harrises had favored.

Her fingers caught at the newel post, held, and she turned her body to look up the long, curving flight of stairs that led to the second floor.

No. She couldn't do that. She wouldn't do that. It was too personal, too private. Looking into a man's bedroom? She couldn't. She just couldn't. Not even Joe's bedroom. *Especially* Joe's bedroom.

He wasn't the black satin sheets type, was he? She didn't think so, hoped not.

Still, she probably ought to check, just to make sure. Only heaven knew what sort of debauched creature he might have turned into after she'd jilted him.

No. She hadn't *jilted* him. Not exactly. Jilted meant she'd left him for someone else, right? She hadn't done that. Okay, so she was marrying Matt next week, but that didn't count. Couldn't count for much. Could it?

"Get a grip, Maddy," she told herself as she climbed the stairs, knowing exactly which was the master bedroom suite. "You're thinking too much, rationalizing stupid moves and now you're talking to yourself. Rubber room, here we come. And yet..."

And yet, what? And yet, she wanted to see Joe's most private space. And yet, she cared enough about him to want him to be happy. And yet, she'd just have to murder him if there was another woman's photograph on his dresser....

There couldn't be another woman. He wouldn't be here if there were another woman. He wouldn't have listened to Allie, bought this house, for crying out loud. He wouldn't be making a bit of a fool of himself, opening himself up to more hurt...not unless he loved. Not unless he really, really loved her.

Ah, rational thought. Wasn't it a blast!

Maybe not, but it got her into his bedroom and, right now, Maddy would content herself with that.

The first thing she saw was herself, an eight-by-ten blown-up photograph of herself from that long-ago day in Atlantic City. There were other pictures. About five of them in different sizes, mostly snapshots; all of them of her, of her with Joe.

Not enough pictures to have him looking like some sort of stalker, but just enough to let her know that he went to sleep looking at the two of them in happier times, that he woke to her smile every morning.

She had many of the same pictures in her room, although she had put them into a drawer once she had Matt's ring on her finger. She still pulled them out, looked at them, traced her fingers over Joe's smiling face, but that was all.

She didn't know if they were both hopeless romantics, or simply pathetic.

She had made her decision, taken the steps necessary to get on with her life, believing that Joe hadn't cared enough, loved enough, to come after her. To persuade her to marry him, be with him. To give up his dream and become her dream of him and how their life should be…

Maddy winced, that particular shaft of insight slicing sharply into her chest. That was it, wasn't it? He was supposed to bend, to agree with her, to become her dream of happily ever after. He wasn't supposed to ask her to leap blindly into a future that could end with the two of them left with nothing but each other.

Nothing but each other. Was that so bad? Was struggling so terrible…or had she run from Joe because she hadn't been able to get him to sit, heel, behave as she felt he should?

"You sure do pick your times, Maddy," she

scolded herself. "These were questions you should have been asking yourself when you were running to cooking classes, instead of running to Philadelphia, running back to Joe, accepting him as he was, accepting yourself as you were."

She walked over to the head of the king-size bed, planning on fixing the bedspread as it lay bunched on top of a pillow. She turned down the spread, picked up the pillow, and was immediately caught by the scent of Joe's aftershave. Her stomach bunched, her eyes closed. And she hugged the pillow close to her. Tears stung her eyes.

There was a slight noise, nothing she could readily put a name to, and she opened her eyes once more, to see Joe standing not ten feet away from her.

He was rubbing a towel over his wet head, and wore another towel low around his waist, a wide smile, and nothing else. His furry chest was still glistening with water droplets and his bare arms and long legs had retained their sculpted Greek god look for the past eighteen months. "To what do I owe this unexpected visit? Have I been a very, very good boy today?" he asked, grinning.

"You…you're…" Maddy threw the pillow back on the bed and pointed a shaking finger at him. "You're not supposed to be here."

"And you are?" Joe asked, taking two steps in her direction.

"Yes! Yes, I am, darn it. I'm here to wait for the cable guy because Allie couldn't do it and…and…" She slapped a hand against her forehead. "Yeah, sure, like Allie would ever volunteer to wait for a cable guy. What was I thinking? Or *not* thinking.

Maybe those pills haven't worn off after all. How could I be so *gullible!*''

"Having a nice conversation with yourself, Maddy?" Joe asked. "Tell you what, let me put some clothes on, and maybe we can do it the old-fashioned way. You know. You talk to me, I talk to you, and we both listen. It would be something new and different for us, of course."

"We have nothing to say to each other," Maddy said, striving to collect herself. "I hate you for coming here and that's all there is to say about anything."

"Except for me to apologize for buying this place out from under you. That was mean, Maddy, and I know it. But you're looking at a desperate man."

She was looking at a near-naked man, and she would have to walk straight past him to get to the door, which was what she was doing. "Apology accepted," she said shortly, raising her chin defiantly. "Now, if you'd please move?"

He stepped back, motioning for her to proceed past him, then he shot out a hand as she did, took hold of her arm at the elbow. "When are you going to tell him, Maddy? Because you have to tell him."

Her arm burned where he touched her. Her chin wobbled as her resolve to leave him standing there fled in a heartbeat. "I'll tell him," she said quietly. "I know I have to tell him. But that doesn't change anything, Joe. I'm still going to marry Matt next week." She turned tear-bright eyes up at him. "Oh, Joe, why couldn't you have let well enough alone?"

He let go of her arm, let her run away, run down the stairs and out of the house. Run all the way home. The front door banged shut behind her and she stopped just inside the foyer, trying to regain her breath.

"Home so soon?" Almira said, walking out from the drawing room.

Maddy narrowed her eyes and glared at her grandmother. "You evil old woman," she growled. "Joe was home. He was in the bathroom, taking a shower. I know, because he came out, wearing nothing but a towel."

"Nothing but a towel? And you were there, waiting for him? Right there in his bedroom?" Almira said, smiling quite happily, and not even bothering to deny her guilt. "Wow, that was even better than I'd hoped for."

"*Aaaargh!*" Maddy screamed, and ran up the stairs.

Chapter Ten

Maddy stood in front of the mirror in her bedroom, dressed in her wedding gown, and thankfully not breaking out in hives. Modern medicine hadn't been able to do anything with her mental turmoil, but at least it had put those itchy hives to bed for a while.

"Take a deep breath, Miss Maddy," Mrs. Ballantine said, attempting to pull up the zipper covered in faux buttons. "I seem to be having a little trouble here."

Maddy looked at her reflection in the mirror, pulled a face. "Is that a polite way of saying, 'Maddy, you're fat?'"

"You're not fat, Maddy," Jessie said, watching as Mrs. Ballantine gave a mighty tug, and got the zipper to go all the way up. "That gown is a size six petite, remember? You're just pleasantly rounded, and in all the right places. Now, *I'm* skinny."

"Yeah, if you say so," Maddy answered. "But I

sure would like to know why I got all the short and fat genes and you got all the tall and thin ones. Oh, I never should have eaten that chocolate cake last night.''

"You made it, you might as well eat it," Jessie said. "Seven layers. *Mmm-mmm*. Maddy, I can't tell you how impressed I am by all your achievements these past years. Even after you came home from college, you still seemed like my baby sister, and not much more. Now? You seem so much more complete now, more your own person. And you've found something you really enjoy, taking care of a house, turning it into a real home. It's like you're some sort of Martha Stewart or something.''

Maddy stood very still while Mrs. Ballantine checked the hem of the gown, inspected her work for any hint of a flaw. "I am pretty good at this home and hearth stuff, aren't I, Jessie? And I really like it, every minute of it. I guess I just wasn't born for the big, bad corporate world. I'd much rather stay home and raise a half-dozen kids.''

"Good," Jessie said. "You can have enough for both of us, as I'll be much too busy working at the plant with Ryan who, by the way, now thinks we should be working twenty-seven hours a day. Personally, I'm beginning to think he wants to bury himself there, at the plant, and not have to be bothered with even pretending to live a real life.''

Maddy looked into the mirror, looked at her sister. "And you'd let him do that? To himself? To *you?*''

Jessie shrugged. "Why not? It's not as if I've got anything else to do with my life, right?''

Maddy was confused. "You mean you're really

going to stick with this career stuff? Never get married or anything?''

Jessie stood up, walked over to the nearest window. ''Prospective grooms aren't exactly kneeling three deep at my feet, Maddy, asking for my hand in marriage.'' At least not the *right* prospective groom...

''There you go, all set,'' Mrs. Ballantine said, unzipping the gown, so that Maddy gratefully let out her breath. ''But I'd stay out of the kitchen between now and Saturday, Miss Maddy. Not that you aren't cute as a button, but I have to say that taking a gown in is a whole lot easier than letting it out. You'll remember that, won't you?''

''Yes, Mrs. Ballantine,'' Maddy said, guiltily remembering the homemade waffles she'd fixed for herself that morning in her own kitchen. Still, she'd eaten them with fresh strawberries, not maple syrup, so how bad could that have been? Pretty bad, obviously, when she considered how uncomfortable her gown had felt a moment ago.

Not that it mattered how the gown felt. It wasn't as if she was going to get to wear it. Not once she got done telling Matt what she had to tell him. Telling Joe what she had to tell him, as well.

''Is Matt coming over this evening?'' Jessie asked, her tone conversational, not at all concerned, or wary. She'd become quite a good actress, accomplished at hiding her feelings these past six months since Matt had proposed and Maddy had accepted.

''Um-hum,'' Maddy said, nodding. She then bent her knees and raised her arms, allowing Mrs. Ballantine to raise the entire gown up and over her head. Once she'd emerged from yards and yards of ivory silk, she asked, ''Are you going to be home? You're never home for dinner anymore. Matt asked me yesterday if you'd run away from home. I mean, when we see Ryan at the dinner table and he tells us you're still at the plant—well, I just wish you'd be here tonight, Jessie, okay?''

Jessie suddenly got the feeling Maddy wanted to use her as some sort of buffer between herself and Matt. ''Is Joe O'Malley invited to dinner tonight, Maddy?'' she asked carefully. ''I wouldn't put it past Allie.''

''Joe?'' Maddy slipped into a pale yellow sundress. ''I have no idea. Not that I could care less.''

Behind her, still struggling with the train of the gown, Mrs. Ballantine snorted, rolled her eyes. ''I'll leave you two girls alone now. To *talk*.''

Jessie watched the housekeeper close the door behind her. ''Okay, what's up? What's going on?''

Maddy bit her upper lip for a moment, the upper lip that had stayed remarkably hive-free, even though she had stopped taking the antihistamines this morning. ''I'm not getting married,'' she said at last, looking at her sister as calmly as she could.

''You're not...you're *not*...'' Jessie hated herself for the way her heart all but jumped out of her chest, probably to hop up and down in glee. ''Ah, Maddy,'' she said, pulling her baby sister into her arms. ''Are you sure?''

Maddy wrapped her arms around her sister's slim waist, nodding her head against Jessie's shoulder. ''I'm sure. I don't know how I'm going to tell Matt, what we're going to do about all the presents, and the caterers, and all that sort of thing. But I can't marry him, Jessie, not when I'm so confused. It wouldn't be fair, not to either of us.''

"Or to Joe," Jessie said, putting her hands on Maddy's shoulders, pushing her slightly away from her. "Would it, Maddy? Be fair to Joe? To Joe, and to you."

Maddy looked down at her shoes. "I want to kill him," she said quietly.

Jessie laughed shortly. "He is rather like a wad of gum on the bottom of your shoe, isn't he? You just can't get rid of him. I think that's because he's in love."

Now it was Maddy's turn to walk to the window, to look out across the way, to the sight of Joe's sparkling blue swimming pool beyond the tall trees. "Is he, Jessie? Am I? I don't know. Maybe he just doesn't like to lose. Maybe I'm just remembering how it was, and forgetting that back then I'd believed what it was was all we could have, that we'd only ruin what was if we kept on with it."

Jessie knitted her brows together, playing over that last statement in her mind. "Could you excuse me a moment, Maddy, while I go get my secret decoder ring? Because I sure need some help deciphering that one."

Maddy turned from the window. "So do I, Jessie," she said with a wan smile. "I don't know about Joe and me, I guess that's what I'm saying. But I do know that having one question, just one niggling question, is reason enough to tell Matt I can't marry him on Saturday."

"Postpone the wedding, you mean."

Maddy shook her head. "No, Jessie, not postpone it. Call it off. And you know what? I think Matt will be relieved. We're friends, good friends, but I think we both knew something was missing. Some sort of spark, you know?''

''And is there a spark with Joe?''

Maddy smiled, sniffed. ''Try a bonfire, Jessie. That would be more like it.'' She twisted her hands together and looked at her sister. ''So, will you be here tonight, Jessie? Will you be here to help me somehow get through dinner, and then wait for me after I tell Matt? I...I think I'm going to need you.''

''Ah, sweetheart,'' Jessie said, gathering the now weeping Maddy into her arms once more. ''Of course I'll be here. You know that. I'll always be here. I just want you to be *sure*.''

''I'm sure,'' Maddy stated as firmly as she could as her chin continued to wobble. ''If I'm sure of nothing else, I'm sure about this.''

''Well, then,'' Jessie said bracingly, trying to put a smile back on her sister's face, ''then let me help you compose a note to Great-Aunt Harriet, telling her how much you regret having to return her lovely gift.''

Maddy looked at her sister. Smiled. Shook her head. ''Ah, Jessie, what would I do without you?''

''You're not going to find out,'' Jessie promised, kissing her sister's cheek, and at the same time remembering that Maddy's future might have changed, but hers had not. She could never let Maddy know that she was secretly in love with her sister's soon-to-be ex-fiancé. ''I just want you to be happy.''

Maddy was up to her elbows in peat moss, bits of it clinging to her ''I'm the gardener'' apron, her bare knees, her scraped-back hair.

She knelt on the edge of the brick path, leaning forward with one arm braced as she swept peat moss around the base of a deep green ornamental grass. The view of her from the back had Joe smiling even as he wondered if he'd be as welcome in Maddy's garden as a plague of locusts.

He'd never seen her like this, not during their whirlwind courtship that had taken place in the middle of the city. But she looked very much at home as a country girl, happy in her own element.

He'd loved her in Philadelphia.

He damn near adored her here in Allentown.

The girl he had met, swept off her feet as she'd swept him off his, had been just that. A girl.

But Maddy was a woman now. He'd broken her heart and she'd run home, but she hadn't stopped living, hadn't become bitter. She'd picked up the pieces and moved on. Taking classes. Finding out who she really was. Becoming engaged to be married.

And what had he done? First, he'd gotten drunk. Stinking drunk. He'd had a real pity party for himself in that hotel room for two days, until Larry flew out to bring him home, remind him of his obligations, offer him work as a cure for what ailed him—*who* ailed him.

On so many levels, Larry's therapy had worked. Joe had worked hard, murderously hard, driving himself to succeed, day in, day out. Driving himself to be better than he was, more than he had been, everything he'd told Maddy he could be. Each morning he woke to her smiling face. He fell into bed at night—on the nights he actually made it to his bed—with her face being the last thing he saw before falling into an exhausted sleep.

Maddy had been the reason for his success. She was the carrot at the end of the stick, the prize at the end of the race. She didn't know; maybe he didn't know it. But she was.

And he'd made it. He'd made it big. Bigger than big. Gigantic. But, funny about that, having it all didn't make him nearly as happy as he'd thought it would. Knowing that Maddy was bound to hear of his success did less than nothing for him.

For months, nearly two years, he had pushed himself so that he could prove to Maddy that she'd been wrong. Rub her nose in it? Damn straight.

Only it hadn't worked. He still had this big, empty space inside. So he'd given up his monklike existence and taken his smiling self out into the society that seemed ready to welcome him with open arms. He met women; lots of women. But he never took them home, never took them to his bed.

Because they weren't Maddy. Nobody else was Maddy. She was one of a kind...and he was a one-woman man.

That was when he'd called the Chandler household, and asked to speak to the woman who'd walked away from him. Not to rub her nose in his success, but to beg her to please, please, let him see her, talk to her, see if they could start over again. Almira Chandler had answered the phone and, as the saying goes...the rest was history.

History. Yes, they had plenty of history, he and Maddy. But did they have a future?

Joe watched as Maddy sat back on her heels, admiring her work, giving a final pat to one area, then slapping her gloves together to rid them of clinging peat moss.

"Very nice, Maddy," he said, wincing as she all but jumped to her feet to glare at him angrily for having surprised her. "I'm sorry. I didn't realize I'd been sneaking up on you." He walked up to her, took out his handkerchief, wiped at a smudge on her left cheek. "God, Mad, but you're beautiful."

He couldn't help himself. He lowered his head, slowly, so as not to frighten her, and pressed his mouth against hers. Gently, barely touching her lips. He kissed her once, twice, then spread his legs slightly, slid one hand behind her head, and pulled her closer, increasing the pressure of his mouth at the same time.

She didn't fight him; couldn't fight him. Maddy just stood there, her eyes fluttering closed, and let him kiss her. And it all came rushing back. The melting heat. The hunger. The wish for his kiss to go on, and on, as he held her until the stars fell and the moon went out.

Joe was near to trembling, finally having Maddy in his arms again. How soft, how warm, how maddening and comforting and exciting and simply wonderful she felt. She was more than his love, his lover. She was *home*.

When the kiss was over, too soon, too soon, Maddy lay her head against Joe's chest, too weak to move away, both physically and emotionally. "You...we shouldn't have done that."

Joe stroked her hair, gave her ponytail a playful tug. "I know. But I'll go to hell if you will."

Now she did push away from him, to look up at

him through tear-filled eyes. "Why, Joe? Why did it take you so long to come after me? Why did you come after me now?"

He pulled a face, tried to lighten the mood. "Lousy timing?" When she frowned, he went on, "Okay, honesty time. Pride. Arrogance, stupidity, stubbornness and pride. I was going to come to you a success on my own terms, or I wasn't going to come to you at all. It was vain, stupid, and anything else you can call it, and I have no excuse for any of it. Not a single day went by without me missing you, and still I didn't come after you. There, is that good enough?"

"Probably," she said, leaning against him again. "If nothing else, it sounds familiar, because I was doing the same thing." She closed her eyes, gave him a quick squeeze, then moved entirely away from him, finally stripping off her filthy gloves. "I've gotten peat moss all over you," she said, stalling for time.

But then she said it; she finally said it: "I have to talk to Matt tonight."

"About us?"

She shot Joe a withering look from beneath her dark lashes. She might love this guy, she might always have loved him, but he sure could rattle her cage. "No, about the charity ball at the hospital next month. Of course, about us. About him and me. That us…and maybe this us—you and me." She scratched an itch on her left forearm and watched as three long white welts appeared as if by magic. "Damn, and I'd better do it soon, or it's back to those antihistamines."

"I'll talk to him," Joe offered, laying a hand on

Maddy's shoulder. "I'll explain, let him know this whole mess is all my fault, and make him understand. Poor guy, he's going to be devastated, isn't he?"

Maddy remembered the previous evening, Matt's chaste kiss on her cheek as they'd said good-night. The rather dark circles under his eyes, his telling her that, for some reason or another, he hadn't been sleeping too well lately. "Is he? Is he really going to be heartbroken, Joe? I sometimes wonder...."

"Now *that*, Mad, is probably just wishful thinking," Joe told her as he walked back down the path, bent to pick up something he'd earlier placed behind the bushes. "Who couldn't love you?"

Maddy smiled weakly. "Thank you, Joe. And thanks for the offer, but I have to do this myself. I owe Matt that. I can't marry him, not when I feel the way I do when I kiss you, you rat. What's in your hand?"

Joe smiled as he deposited the large, gaily wrapped container in front of her, letting go of the handle that stuck out through the paper. "I was coming over to try to talk to you," he admitted rather sheepishly. "And I figured I might make more progress, and be safer, if I'd arrived bearing a gift. Do you want to open it?"

Swiping at another, unexpected bout of tears, Maddy looked down at the wrappings. "It looks as if somebody already started to unwrap it. There are holes in the paper on every side. You wrapped this, you say? My, how nice it is to know that the great J. P. O'Malley doesn't excel at everything."

There was a sound from within the wrapping paper, and the box seemed to shift slightly on the uneven bricks. Maddy stepped back a pace. "Joe? What's in there?"

"I can see I'm going to have to do this myself," he said, and ripped off the wrapping with one good pull, exposing a gray plastic pet carrier. He reached inside and pulled out a small ball of orange fur, holding it up so Maddy could see.

"A kitten?" Maddy tipped her head to one side, watching as the small animal moved all four legs frantically, opened its mouth to show tiny sharp teeth and a pinker than pink tongue. "You brought me a *kitten?*"

Joe shrugged, handing the kitten to her, stepping back to watch as the animal immediately settled down in her arms, began to purr. Maddy stroked the cat's head with one finger and the kitten immediately raised his head, began to lick her fingertip. Even a kitten knew when he had a good thing going, Joe supposed. "It's the present for the woman who has everything. Or, if you want, we can call it an engagement present. Will you marry me, Maddy— again?"

"Why did she *do* that?" Mrs. Ballantine asked, turning away from the upstairs window, reaching into her pocket for her handkerchief. "Why did she hand him the kitten and run into the house? I don't understand."

Almira sighed, let the curtain fall back into place and walked over to sit down on the antique fainting couch her husband had given her for their thirtieth anniversary. "I don't know," she said quietly. "Was I wrong, Lucille? I know she doesn't love

Matt, but does she really still love Joe? Did she ever really love Joe? Have I ruined everything?''

Lucille Ballantine gave up on all her professional distance and sat herself down beside her employer. ''I don't know, Almira,'' she said, putting an arm around the smaller woman's shoulders. ''Maybe marrying a friend is better than marrying for love. All that passion, things like that—very wearing on a person, you know. Passion, that is. I know.''

Almira looked up at Mrs. Ballantine. ''Lucille, you never said,'' she teased halfheartedly. ''Tell me more. Tell me about all the passion in your life. Was Mr. Ballantine a very passionate man?''

''There never was a Mr. Ballantine,'' Lucille said, rising from the couch to adjust the curtains Almira had not arranged to her satisfaction. ''It was just easier letting everyone think there had been one, once.''

''Well, I'll be damned,'' Almira said, shaking her head. ''Here I am, reading books, and here it is, all this romance and intrigue going on right under my nose, and I don't know it. There was a sad love affair, Lucille, wasn't there?''

''No sadder than most. We met, we fell in love, we fought and he married someone else. The last time I heard anything about Barney, he was on his fourth wife.'' She smiled wryly. ''I like to think he's spent all of his life looking for someone to replace me. And failing.''

Almira nodded sagely. ''And now I know why you were so willing to help me, Lucille. You don't want to see Maddy making the same mistakes your Barney did. You knew, as I did, that Matthew Garvey is a wonderful man, but he could never be more than a substitute for Joe O'Malley, no matter how hard he tried. Especially when I don't think his heart is in this marriage any more than Maddy's is."

As if saying her name conjured her up, Maddy blew into her grandmother's sitting room and looked from Allie to Lucille, her hands drawn up into fists. "I just want you two to know that I'm going to tell Matt tonight that I can't marry him. So, whatever else you're planning and plotting about up here—and I'm sure there's *something*—you can just stop it, now."

"Why didn't you take the kitten?" Almira asked, as Maddy's first statement really didn't require an answer. The girl knew she'd come to the conclusion her grandmother had wished for her, and trying to argue at this late date that she *hadn't* been meddling? Well, that would just be ridiculous.

"Why didn't I—you two were *watching?* Oh, oh, I don't believe this!" Maddy turned herself in a full circle, then glared at both women. "Yes, I do. I'd probably believe anything you two would do. *Spying* on me, Allie? Aren't you ashamed of yourselves?"

Almira looked at Mrs. Ballantine. "Are you ashamed of yourself, Lucille? I'm not." As the housekeeper shook her head slightly, Almira smiled at her granddaughter. "Nope. We're not ashamed of ourselves. So, why did you kiss him, and then not accept the kitten? There was a bow on the box, so we already know it was a present."

Maddy might be nearing the end of her emotional rope, but she wasn't so desperate or so upset that she'd tell her grandmother that Joe had asked her to marry him even before she could give back Matt's ring. That she had hated him at that moment, even as she loved him, loved him more than she really should, most probably. As Joe had said, sometimes he had some really lousy timing.

"I'm allergic to cats," she said at last, daring her grandmother to contradict her.

Never dare Almira Chandler. That rule should probably be carved into the drawing room mantelpiece. "You are not. You had a kitten when you were younger. Fluffy, I think you named the poor thing. Horrible name for such a proud animal. Now, try again, dear. Did he ask you to marry him? That's what I would have done."

"You would," Maddy exclaimed, shaking her head. "You and Joe are a real pair. Can't we at least let the body cool before we start picking out new china patterns? Can't you understand how *guilty* I'm feeling right now?"

"Do you want me to tell Matt?" Almira offered.

"*No,* I do *not* want you to tell him. I don't want Joe to tell him. What is this, anyway? Doesn't anyone believe I can handle this? Am I so incompetent I can't have a perfectly normal, if difficult, conversation with Matt?"

"Well…" Almira began, looking to Mrs. Ballantine. "No. No, of course. You're right, Maddy. It's time we all took a step back, and let you handle your own life. I'm only sorry I interfered. I had no right. Really."

Maddy looked at her grandmother, finally saw the age behind the cosmetic surgery and her heart softened. "You may be sorry, Allie, but I'm not. You've done both Matt and me a big favor."

"And Joe?"

Maddy's smile faded. "I don't know, Allie. I just don't know…."

Chapter Eleven

Ryan closed the car trunk on his golf bag and turned to Matt. "This was a good idea you had, old pal. Although it probably wasn't fair of you to bet me a quarter a hole when you know I hadn't been on a golf course yet this year."

Matt grinned, putting his hand into his pocket and jingling the change. "I'll invest it all wisely, I promise," he said, clapping Ryan on the shoulder as they headed back to the club to have sandwiches and drinks in the Grille. "But I have to tell you, this wasn't my idea, although I wished I'd had it. Jessie phoned me at the bank and suggested I get you out into the sunlight and fresh air before you turned into a dry old stick. Are you in danger of turning into a dry old stick, Ryan?"

Totally oblivious to the smile and longing look of the waitress directed at him as they passed her on their way into the Grille, Ryan pushed a hand through his coal-black hair, shook his head. "Just old, Matt. Just old. But you know how it is. Work's something we never seem to run out of.''

''I suppose,'' Matt said, sitting down across from his friend. ''But don't you think you're overdoing it? Jessie says you're working seven days a week now. As your banker, I thank you, because I love servicing your accounts. As your friend...well, maybe you ought to think about taking a small vacation.''

''Hi, Ryan.'' The blonde who'd approached their table leaned a hip against it and smiled down at him. She was wearing tennis whites above her long, straight legs, and a smile that said a lot more than hello. ''Hi, Matt,'' she added belatedly.

''How are you doing, Melissa?'' Ryan said as he and Matt rose from their chairs, being the polite men they had been born to be, even if Ryan was wishing Melissa Gerhart somewhere in Siberia at the moment. ''I'm sorry I couldn't return your call.''

''Calls, darling. Plural.'' Melissa ran one red-tipped nail down the length of Ryan's arm. ''So, have you decided to escort me to Matt's wedding to your little sister?''

''I'll call you later,'' he promised, then sat down as Melissa pouted, then walked away. ''You had to go and get married, didn't you?'' he said accusingly to Matt. ''Matt?'' he continued as his friend didn't smile, but just took a drink of his beer and looked past him, right over his shoulder. ''Hey, Mattie, boy. What's wrong?''

''Wrong?'' Matt repeated. ''There's nothing... well, maybe I haven't been sleeping too well.''

''Prewedding jitters?'' Ryan prodded. ''That's okay. I'm the best man, remember? I'll get you to the church on time, or the backyard, as this is a garden wedding.''

Matt reached up a hand, scratched at a spot behind his ear. ''That's not it, Ryan. It's...it's...'' He dropped his hand, held both out in front of himself for a moment. ''No. That's not why we're here. We're here to get you out for some fresh air. Tell me again how you decided to use a three wood out of that trap on Sixteen.''

''Another time, buddy,'' Ryan said shortly. ''What's going on? Did you and Maddy have a fight?''

Matt smiled sadly. ''Nope. No fight. We've never fought. I don't think we'd know how. As a matter of fact, we don't do much of anything. We're just sort of...*polite* to each other.''

Ryan shifted in his chair. ''Since when?''

''Since the beginning,'' Matt answered before taking another sip of beer. ''You know, that's how it started out. Talking, finding out we had a lot in common. We both want to settle down, have a home, kids. We sort of just *drifted* into the rest of it.''

''And this is a bad thing?'' Ryan asked carefully.

''I didn't think so,'' Matt said, hardly believing he was having this conversation. ''But do you know what? I can feel more electricity between Maddy and J. P. O'Malley than I can between Maddy and myself. And she hardly knows him.''

Ryan choked on his sip of beer. Coughed. ''Yeah...well...'' What else could he say? Plenty, once he got home and cornered Maddy. She had to talk to Matt, tell him about Joe O'Malley. Now. Before one more day passed on the way to this wedding that was beginning to sound like a really bad idea—on *both* sides.

In the meantime, he had to ask. He really had to ask. "Matt, do you love my sister?"

Matt rubbed at his mouth as he looked across the table at his friend. It had to be said. Sooner or later, it had to be said. "Yes, Ryan, I do. I'm just not engaged to marry her."

Jessie was pacing in the drawing room when Ryan walked in only a few minutes before six. "You're late," she said accusingly. "Linda Garvey will be here any minute. Allie asked her to be here, which was probably a good idea—I'll explain that later. Did you go back to work?"

"I did have a few things to finish up," he said, kissing his sister's cheek. "What's the matter, you look sort of…flustered. No, that couldn't be. You never fluster, do you, Jessie?"

She looked at him oddly, because his remarks were odd. Totally out of character. "Maybe we're both working too hard, Ryan. Do we really have to do that?"

Ryan loosened his tie, sat down on one of the sofas. "No, I suppose we don't."

She sat down beside him. "Then why do we?"

He picked up her hand, gave it a squeeze. "I think I know why you do, Jess. Do you want to tell me about it? About Matt?"

Jessie didn't know what she had been expecting from her brother, but it certainly hadn't been this. She leaped to her feet, walked over to pour them both glasses of water. "You're my brother, Ryan, not some father confessor. However, if you want to tell me why you're so damn dedicated to killing yourself at the plant, please feel free.''

''Okay, so it's a draw,'' Ryan agreed, accepting the glass. ''Where is everybody?''

''Allie says she has a headache, and will eat in her rooms, if you can believe that. She's never sick. And Linda will be here any moment, as I told you. She had some last-minute emergency at the office. And...and Matt and Maddy are out in the garden. Talking.''

''Just what I didn't want, front row seats,'' Ryan muttered under his breath as he sliced a look toward the French doors that were open to catch the light June breeze. ''Interesting. And Joe O'Malley? Where's he?''

Joe was in his own living room, pacing. This was it. Tonight had to be the night. Maddy was going to tell Matt she couldn't marry him. She hadn't actually said so, but he knew Maddy. It might take her a while to make up her mind, but once she did, she acted.

He stopped pacing, looked down to see the orange kitten rubbing up against his pants cuff. Smiling, he bent down, picked up the animal, and held it up to him, face-to-face. ''She wouldn't keep you, would she, boy? But don't worry, it's only temporary. It's me we've got to worry about, especially if you want me around. Do you want me around, Tiger?''

The kitten began to purr and Joe pressed his nose to the animal's before putting it back on the carpet, where it immediately sat down and began cleaning itself.

And Joe went back to his wondering....

She hadn't said no. She hadn't said yes, but she hadn't said no. That had to mean something.

And his timing could have been better. A whole hell of a lot better.

Like, eighteen months ago, when he should have run after her, never have let her get away from him in the first place.

Like, eight months ago, when the first wave of his new software had hit, and he and Larry had known they were about to become the next overnight sensations of the computer software world.

Or five months ago, when he had finally gotten over his exhaustion, and his pride, and acknowledged that success meant absolutely nothing without Maddy there to share in it with him. Larry had told him to make up his mind, and for God's sake make his move, or to just shut up about Maddy and get on with his life. He should have listened to the man.

Thinking of Larry...the man was upstairs now, probably showering, probably singing loudly in the shower, and expecting to be taken out to dinner later. *Lots of luck, Lar,* Joe thought, knowing he wasn't taking a single step from this house until he heard from Maddy. *If* he heard from Maddy.

He *had* to hear from Maddy....

"...and that's just about it. I thought I was over him, really, really thought I was over him, but I'm not. And, since I'm not, it wouldn't be fair to marry you. You can see that, can't you? I'm sorry I never told you, Matt. I should have. But I really thought I was over him. Really. Even now I sometimes want to kill him. Except that I love him." Maddy took a deep breath, let it out slowly. "I really do love him. I'm so, so sorry."

Matt sat beside Maddy on a wrought-iron bench in the garden, his elbows on his knees, his fingers laced together. He had his head slightly bowed as he looked down at the bricks at his feet. Maddy couldn't know it, but he was smiling.

"Matt?" Maddy put a hand on his shoulder. "Are you all right? Say something, Matt. *Please.* Say something, Matt, you're scaring me."

He couldn't do it. He couldn't pretend, lie to her, look at her without smiling. J. P. O'Malley. Hell, he should have known—maybe he had known, somehow. He sat up, pulled Maddy against his chest, kissed the top of her head. "I love you, Maddy Chandler. God bless you, you've made me the happiest man in the world."

Maddy stiffened in his arms. She hadn't known what response she'd been expecting, but it certainly hadn't been this. "I did?" Her eyes were wide as she dumbly stared past his shoulder, into the wall of roses behind her. "How did I do that?"

Matt laughed at her question, pushing her away from him. "Ah, Maddy, it was never right, was it? We agreed to the marriage for all the wrong reasons. *Good* reasons, but not the *best* reasons. You're probably not going to believe this, but I agreed to come out here in the garden with you so I could tell you I wanted to postpone the wedding. No, not postpone. Cancel the wedding. You deserve more than I can give you, Maddy. I've been thinking that for a while now. And if J. P. O'Malley can give that happiness to you, hey, I say go for it."

After spending a very long, nervous afternoon,

preparing her speech, rehearsing that speech, to have Matt agree to canceling their wedding so quickly, so easily, so, according to him, *happily,* had come as quite a surprise. "And the presents? The guests? All the rest of it?"

"I'll take care of everything, Maddy," Matt said. "Everyone will know that you've had second thoughts, and that poor old me is devastated, but carrying on the best I can. All right? The idea of everyone being nice to me, dripping sympathy all over me, is cheering me up already."

Maddy stood, clapped her hands to either side of her head. "I don't believe this, Matt! You *don't* want to marry me? You were going to tell me that tonight? You don't want to marry me?"

"You're not in love with me, Maddy," he reminded her, also standing, slipping an arm around her shoulders.

"Well yes, I *know* that," she said, realizing that she might be becoming just a teensy bit unreasonable. "But...but...are you really telling me the truth? I'd feel so much better if you said you were in love with someone else, or couldn't stand the way I cook, or that my conversation bored you, or...or *something.* But you just don't love me?"

"I *do* love you, Maddy, darling. I'm just not *in love* with you. Just as you aren't in love with me. I was your second choice. I didn't know that then, but I know it now. And that's all right, honestly."

"Because I was *your* second choice?" Maddy asked, looking at him intently. She still couldn't tell if he was telling her the truth or simply trying to make her feel better.

"No, Maddy," Matt said, kissing her cheek so

that she couldn't see his eyes. The last thing he wanted Maddy to know was that he had somehow fallen in love with her sister. Sometime between putting the ring on Maddy's finger and two or so weeks ago, he had stupidly, hopelessly fallen in love with a woman who, like his sister, had no intention of marrying anyone, ever.

"I just thought we could both be happier if we waited until we met someone who drove us crazy, Maddy, kept us up all night, and made us eager to wake up every morning. You've got that with J. P. O'Malley, I can see it in your eyes. I should have seen it sooner, frankly. And I'm glad, Maddy, I'm really happy for you. More than you can know."

Maddy still needed to nail all this down in her mind. "You're not upset."

"Nope."

"You're not heartbroken."

"Not at all."

"You're not just trying to make me feel better. You won't suffer."

"Do you want me to suffer?"

"No! No, of course not. You're happy, and that's good. Man, if this isn't something! Allie invited Linda here tonight for dinner, because she thought it might be a good idea," Maddy admitted, wincing. "But I guess you're not going to need her around to offer you a shoulder to cry on or anything like that, are you? You know, I'm beginning to think I should be insulted. But I'm not."

Matt threw back his head and laughed. "God, but I love you Chandlers!" he exclaimed. "Linda? Here? How did you tear her away from her patients? No, wait—does she already know?"

Maddy plucked at a small leaf that had landed on her blouse somehow. "Well...*actually*...now that you mention it. I had all those hives, remember, and she is my doctor. And really, really good at worming out stuff I'd rather not say to her."

Matt gave Maddy's shoulder another squeeze. He was almost sorry he'd confided in Ryan that afternoon, but he was sure he could count on his best friend going along with anything he said—even if he would ask a dozen pointed questions later. His sister certainly had come here tonight ready to pity him. And Jessie? Who ever knew what Jessie was thinking? Certainly not him.

They'd pull it off. He, Ryan, Linda. For Maddy's sake, Ryan wouldn't let on that he knew Matt was going to end the engagement tonight. Linda was like the Sphinx, so there were no worries there of her mentioning J.P. in any way at all.

And, although he was sure Jessie had known about J.P., she couldn't know that he, Matt, had been planning on calling off the wedding. Why, she might even feel sympathetic toward him, want to comfort him. He could drink a little all through dinner, act the brave but hurt ex-groom, take her sympathy if that was all he could get.

He could live with that.

Lord, he was pathetic....

"Come on, Maddy, let's go back to the house. Suddenly I'm very hungry. But remember. Subdued, as we have a nice, civilized dinner. We'll let them all think you dumped me. Nicely, but that you dumped me just the same. I mean, hey, Ryan might even give me two strokes on him next time we play golf, just because he's feeling sorry for me."

"I love you, Matt Garvey," Maddy said in all sincerity as they made their way back to the house, arm in arm.

"But you'll be leaving me now, to go next door and give J.P. a blow-by-blow, right?"

"Wrong," Maddy said as she slipped the emerald cut diamond from her hand and slipped it into Matt's pocket. "After all he's put me through? I think we're just going to let him stew in his own juices a while longer."

"Always the gourmet cook, Maddy," Matt said, standing back so that she could enter the drawing room ahead of him. "Here we go. Here's where I earn my Oscar, you fickle heartbreaker you."

There was something very wrong with this picture.

He'd watched, shamelessly, from his attic window as Maddy and Matt walked into the garden, then cursed as the covering trees hid them from his view.

He'd watched as they'd walked back to the house, arm in arm.

Which meant that either Matt Garvey was up for the Nice Guy of the Year award, or Maddy hadn't told him.

So he'd gone back downstairs, gone back to his pacing.

After an hour of that, and deciding that pacing was getting him nowhere, he sat down on the couch, stared at his hands.

And thought.

Was this how he'd gotten to the top of the career ladder? By being passive? By letting someone else do his talking for him? By being afraid to walk in, tell it like it is, and the hell with the consequences?

Was he Joey O'Malley from South Philly, or was he Joseph the Worm, letting his woman do his dirty work for him? A woman who, for all he knew, was caught between loving him and wanting his head on a stick.

"I'm outta here!" he told the carpet as he slapped his hands against his knees, stood up. Headed for the door.

A minute later he was knocking on the door across the way, shifting from foot to foot like a prizefighter as he waited for someone to open up and let him in. Let him get on with it.

Mrs. Ballantine opened the door, still looking back over her shoulder as she did so. Without looking at him, she said, "Good evening, Mr. O'Malley. The family is at dinner. You…um…you might want to go away, come back later?"

Joe pushed the door completely open as he walked inside the foyer. "Hello, Almira," he said to the woman standing halfway down the stairs. "What's the matter? Are things so screwed up that you had to send Mrs. Ballantine to get rid of me? And you're not *at dinner* with the family, are you? Want to tell me why?"

"Mr. O'Malley, I really think you should—"

"Oh, don't bother, Lucille," Almira said, coming the rest of the way down the stairs, trailing her ivory silk dressing gown behind her. "I'm a big girl now, and capable of facing up to my own mistakes." She took Joe's arm and led him into the smaller drawing room on the opposite side of the center hallway.

"Joe, my dear boy, I may have overplayed my

hand—our hand, actually. Yes, I've successfully convinced Maddy that marriage to Matt Garvey would be a huge mistake. Yes, she's going to tell him she can't marry him. But, in doing so, I may also have ruined any chance you have to get her back. You do want her back, don't you?''

"No, Almira," Joe said as he glared at the woman. "I buy a mansion a week. Come crawling after a woman engaged to another man, just on the off chance she might still love me, want me. It's just something I do.''

"Don't be sarcastic, Joe, that won't help." Almira sat down, motioned for Joe to do so as well. He ignored the gesture. "I think," she continued, then sighed, shook her head. "I *think* you'd better stay away from Maddy for a while, let her calm down. She loves you, I'm still sure of that, but you aren't her favorite person right now. And, yes, I think that's my fault. I meddled. I shouldn't have done that.''

Mrs. Ballantine entered the room, carrying a small silver tray with two glasses of white wine on it. "She's been blaming herself all day, Mr. O'Malley. Between us, we've decided that Miss Maddy is about the unhappiest happy woman we've ever seen. So it might be best if you were to go home now, come back tomorrow. Or just wait for Miss Maddy to come to you.''

"The hell I will!" Joe said, already halfway out the door, and on his way through the foyer, in search of the dining room. So he didn't see Mrs. Ballantine hand one glass to Almira, keep the other for herself.

"That should about do it, Lucille," Almira said as the two clinked their glasses together in a toast.

"Care to join me in the dining room? I think this should be fun."

So Almira and Mrs. Ballantine were only a few paces behind Joe as he entered the dining room.

The scene that met Joe's eyes when he banged open the double doors was enough to make him wonder if he'd somehow stepped into the Twilight Zone.

Ryan Chandler sat at the head of the long table, Jessica Chandler at its foot. That was reasonable enough.

But there was Maddy, sitting next to Matt on one side of the table, and there was Larry Barry and some woman he'd never seen before, sitting on the other side.

They'd all stopped their conversations as the double doors banged against the wall, looking at Joe as if he'd come in wearing an Indian headdress or had forgotten his slacks.

"Larry?" Joe questioned blankly, belatedly realizing he'd forgotten all about the man. "What in hell...?"

Larry, dapper in his blue suit, his gray temples and gold-rimmed glasses giving him a mature, trustworthy gentleman of the world appearance, looked at Joe for a moment, then turned to his host. "You can take the boy out of South Philly," he said, sighing theatrically, "but you can't always take the South Philly out of the boy, much as I've tried." Then he turned back to Joe. "Were you invited? I don't think you were invited."

"And *you* were?" Joe asked, looking at Maddy, who was sitting quite at ease beside the man whose heart she was supposed to have broken earlier that evening.

"I invited him," Almira said from behind Joe. "As I didn't think you should be here tonight, I thought it would be a simple way of evening out the numbers. I never liked having an odd number at my dinner table."

Joe stood very still, the index finger of his right hand tapping back and forth like a metronome between Larry and Almira, ticking along with his thoughts. Larry, Almira. Almira, Larry. And, slowly, he smelled a rat. "How long has this been going on?"

"How long?" Larry repeated, patting his lips with his napkin, then getting to his feet. "Oh, I don't know. Almira, how long has this been going on?"

Now Maddy was on her feet, saying nothing, watching everything, and slowly figuring out that she hadn't been the only one who'd been maneuvered like a pawn on a chess board. "Allie?" she said hesitantly, then went silent when Matt put his hand on her forearm, shook his head to tell her she might want to just stand back and watch a while longer.

Joe was also thinking. Thinking back over the past months, and all the times Maddy's name had somehow cropped up in Larry's conversations with him. Oblique references to the "old days." Odd times when Larry would seem to fall into reminiscences of the times he and Joe and Maddy would stay up until dawn, Maddy running out for sandwiches and coffee as Joe worked at the computer and Larry crunched numbers.

A plot. It had all been a plot. Almira Chandler and his best friend. Plotting against him.

No, wait. Plotting *for* him. For him, and for Maddy.

"Well, I'll be damned," he said at last, grinning sheepishly as he ran a hand through his hair. "Maddy, we've been had." He walked around the table, stood beside Matt's chair. "She told you, didn't she?"

Matt pushed back his chair, stood up. "Yes, she did."

"And you two broke off the engagement?"

"We did," Matt answered as Maddy slipped her hand into his, squeezed it. He didn't have to act the disappointed groom at this point. He was too busy figuring out that Almira Chandler had never seen him as husband material for her granddaughter. Did she feel the same way about both her granddaughters? He'd thought Almira liked him. He must have been wrong. "I've already promised Maddy that I'd handle everything, make all the necessary phone calls."

Joe held out his hand, shook Matt's. "I'm sorry you had to be caught in the middle of this, Matt."

"Don't be," Matt said shortly. "I think we've all been playing the puppet as Almira worked the strings. Now, if you'll all excuse me?"

"Matt! Wait for me!" Jessie exclaimed, jumping out of her chair, and taking only a moment to glare at her brother. "Think retirement homes in Florida, Ryan. Think about them now!" Then, with only a glance at her grandmother, she ran after Matt.

Which left Maddy and Joe staring at each other.

"Are you all right?" he asked her.

"I think so," Maddy answered dully, then straightened her shoulders, her spine. "So? Have we gone through all of this again because of Allie and Loony—I mean, because of Larry—just to end up where we were before? Are we really in love, Joe, or have we only been manipulated into thinking that way?"

Joe took both her hands in his. "What do you think, Maddy?"

Ryan motioned for everyone else to follow him as he led the way out of the room, leaving Maddy and Joe still standing there, still looking at each other.

"Maddy? Will you forgive me for not chasing after you?"

"If you'll forgive me for running away, for not having faith in you."

"Would you really have married him? If I hadn't shown up, would you have married Matt Garvey?"

Maddy bit her lips together, shook her head. "No." She looked up at Joe. "Somewhere deep inside my head, I knew it was wrong. I wasn't happy, Matt wasn't happy. We just didn't know what to do about it."

"I did!" Almira said, poking her head back into the dining room, just to have a red-tipped and very white hand clamp down on her shoulder, pulling her back out again.

"I'm sorry about that," Mrs. Ballantine said, sticking her head inside the door. "You two just pretend that didn't happen. I'll be sure you aren't interrupted again."

Maddy and Joe nodded at the housekeeper, then looked at each other. Smiled. Began to laugh.

Fell into each other's arms, laughing so hard they practically had to hold each other up.

Until Joe sobered, pushed Maddy slightly away from him and looked deeply into her tear-bright eyes. "I love you, Maddy. I have loved you since the first time I saw you. I will love you ten years after I'm dead. Please, Maddy. Marry me. There— is my timing finally right?"

She never did get to say, "yes," to any of his questions, because Joe kissed her then, kissed her long and hard and with the intention of never, never ever, letting her go again.

* * * * *

Chapter One

"Do you think she'll find him?"

Almira looked at Mrs. Ballantine as they both let the curtains fall back into place and turned away from the window overlooking the rear gardens, lit only by the full moon. "She's my granddaughter, Lucille. Of course she'll find him."

"Did you see his face when he realized that you'd been plotting to stop his wedding to Miss Maddy? I think he believes you don't like him. I really felt sorry for him, poor man. And sorry I let you get me mixed up in all of this."

"Are you sorry, Lucille? Really sorry? After all, we've already got Maddy and Joe settled. We're one for one. Although I must admit there were moments when I wished we'd handled things differently. Especially when poor Maddy started breaking out in hives. So maybe we'll just leave Jessie and Matt to their own devices. They are, after all, two distinctly different personalities than Maddy and Joe."

"And Miss Jessie is even more stubborn and proud than Miss Maddy," Mrs. Ballantine pointed out, picking up her glass and taking a sip of wine. It had been a long day, and she wasn't about to fall back on ceremony at this point. "Almira, I think we're done now. It's time to let your grandchildren settle themselves."

Almira looked toward the window, then took a sip of her wine. "We'll see, Lucille. We'll see…"

Matthew Garvey's car was still in the driveway, so Jessie was pretty sure he was still on the grounds. She didn't call his name, but walked slowly to the back of the house, taking her time as her eyes adjusted to the near-dark. "Matt?" she questioned quietly, thinking she saw the outline of his body inside the gazebo.

"Jessie?" he responded, walking to the entrance to the gazebo, holding out his hand to her as she climbed the three short steps.

He'd been drinking during dinner. Not enough to get drunk, but definitely enough to allow himself to get needlessly maudlin as he'd looked down the table at Jessie, knowing she hadn't the slightest idea how much he loved her, seeing the sympathy in her huge blue eyes. He could stand anything, except her sympathy.

Still, he'd had hope. Or at least he had until he realized that Almira Chandler had gone to extraordinarily great lengths to get rid of him as a prospective grandson-in-law. That hurt. Sure, he and Maddy had been wrong, almost from the beginning, but to have Almira all but turn the world on its head in order to make sure they wouldn't marry? That went beyond assuring her granddaughter's happiness; it was insulting.

After all, she could have come to *him*. If Maddy hadn't intended to tell him about J. P. O'Malley, then Almira could have taken him into her confidence. It sure would have made these last weeks easier....

"Are you all right?" Jessie asked, sitting down on one of the cushioned chaises, pulling him down next to her. "That was so *cruel* of Allie. Especially after you'd been so wonderful about Maddy, so much the gentleman, even when you had to be shocked and unhappy. I didn't realize how hurtful this all must be to you, and I don't think Allie did, either—not until all the color seemed to run out of your face. Please accept my apologies, from all of us."

Matt smiled crookedly. "I'll live," he said, trying for some levity. After all, he wasn't exactly heartbroken by his broken engagement. Just hurt to know Almira's low opinion of him.

Jessie's heart was breaking for him. Breaking for herself, as she knew that Matt wouldn't be coming to the Chandler house anymore, probably finding it easier to visit with Ryan elsewhere, away from the memories of this night.

She put her hand on his arm, leaned closer, smelled the sweet odor of scotch on his breath. "I wish...I wish there was something else I could say...something else I could do..."

Aw, hell. Maybe it was the drink. Maybe it was everything that had happened in so short a time. Maybe he was just a louse, and ready to grab with both hands what he knew in his heart would never be offered again.

He turned on the chaise, put his hands on Jessie's shoulders. Pulled her closer to him. Closer...

Jessie slept deeply in her bed, her dreams of Matt alone able to penetrate the edges of her mind. If the images had become more vivid, she wouldn't have been able to sleep at all. Not after what she'd done tonight, what she'd allowed...what she'd encouraged.

Turning onto her back, she sighed in her sleep as her left hand stirred on the sheets, moved to rest, fingers splayed, on her flat stomach.

And within Jessie's womb, in its earliest stages of being, a tiny, childlike voice whispered to her, *Hello....*

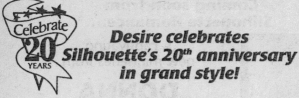

USA Today Bestselling Author

SHARON SALA

has won readers' hearts with thrilling tales
of romantic suspense. Now Silhouette Books
is proud to present five passionate stories from
this beloved author.

Available in August 2000:
ALWAYS A LADY
A beauty queen whose dreams have been dashed in a
tragic twist of fate seeks shelter for her wounded spirit
in the arms of a rough-edged cowboy....

Available in September 2000:
GENTLE PERSUASION
A brooding detective risks everything to protect the
woman he once let walk away from him....

Available in October 2000:
SARA'S ANGEL
A woman on the run searches desperately for a reclusive
Native American secret agent—the only man who can save
her from the danger that stalks her!

Available in November 2000:
HONOR'S PROMISE
A struggling waitress discovers she is really a rich heiress—
and must enter a powerful new world of wealth and
privilege on the arm of a handsome stranger....

Available in December 2000:
KING'S RANSOM
A lone woman returns home to the ranch where she was
raised, and discovers danger—as well as the man she once
loved with all her heart....

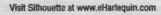

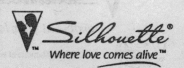

Silhouette invites you to come back to Whitehorn, Montana...

MONTANA MAVERICKS

WED IN WHITEHORN—
12 BRAND-NEW stories that capture living and loving beneath the Big Sky where legends live on and love lasts forever!

M M

June 2000—
Lisa Jackson *Lone Stallion's Lady* (#1)

July 2000—
Laurie Paige *Cheyenne Bride* (#2)

August 2000—
Jennifer Greene *You Belong to Me* (#3)

September 2000—
Victoria Pade *The Marriage Bargain* (#4)

And the adventure continues...

Available at your favorite retail outlet.

Silhouette ROMANCE™

COMING NEXT MONTH

#1474 THE ACQUIRED BRIDE—Teresa Southwick
Storkville, USA
Single mother Dana Hewitt would do anything to keep her
kids—even agree to a convenient marriage with tycoon
Quentin McCormack! But then she began dreaming of being
his real bride—in every sense of the word....

#1475 JESSIE'S EXPECTING—Kasey Michaels
The Chandlers Request...
Sweet Jessie Chandler had always loved Matthew Garvey from
afar. But he had never noticed her—until an innocent kiss led to
an unexpected night of passion. What would Matthew's reaction
be once he learned Jessie's expecting?

#1476 SNOWBOUND SWEETHEART—Judy Christenberry
The Circle K Sisters
When city gal Lindsay Crawford became snowbound with
handsome rancher Gil Daniels, she couldn't help falling for him.
But he thought she wouldn't be happy with country living forever.
Could she convince him that her home was where *he* was?

#1477 THE NANNY PROPOSAL—Donna Clayton
Single Doctor Dads
Greg Hamilton had his hands full raising his ten-month-old baby,
and Jane Dale's motherly touch was just what the doctor ordered.
Although Greg wasn't looking for a wife, seeing his pretty nanny
rocking his baby triggered some unsettling feelings in his bachelor
heart....

#1478 RAISING BABY JANE—Lilian Darcy
Allie Todd had vowed never to get close to another man again. Yet
sharing close quarters with Connor Callahan while caring for her
six-month-old niece had forged a bond between them that couldn't
be denied—just like the secret she was keeping about the maternity
of baby Jane....

#1479 ONE FIANCÉE TO GO, PLEASE—Jackie Braun
To secure the job of his dreams, Jack Maris asked Tess Donovan to
pose as his fiancée. Savoring the distraction from her demanding
life, Tess agreed. But when word of their engagement spread, they
kept up the charade. And then things got deliciously complicated....

CMN0900